72%
Match

72%
Match

Online Dating Works... Right?

Dalia Lance
&
Raymond Cloose

4 Horsemen Publications

72% Match
Copyright © 2020-2024 Dalia Lance and Raymond Cloose. All rights reserved.

4 Horsemen
Publications, Inc.

Published By: 4 Horsemen Publications, Inc.

4 Horsemen Publications, Inc.
PO Box 417
Sylva, NC 28779
4horsemenpublications.com
info@4horsemenpublications.com

Cover & Typesetting by Valerie Willis
Editor Tilda M. Cooke

Paperback ISBN-13: 978-1-64450-062-0
Hardcover ISBN-13: 979-8-8232-0704-1
Audiobook ISBN-13: 978-1-64450-036-1
Ebook ISBN-13: 978-1-64450-000-2

For the Chrissys and Schuylers of the world.

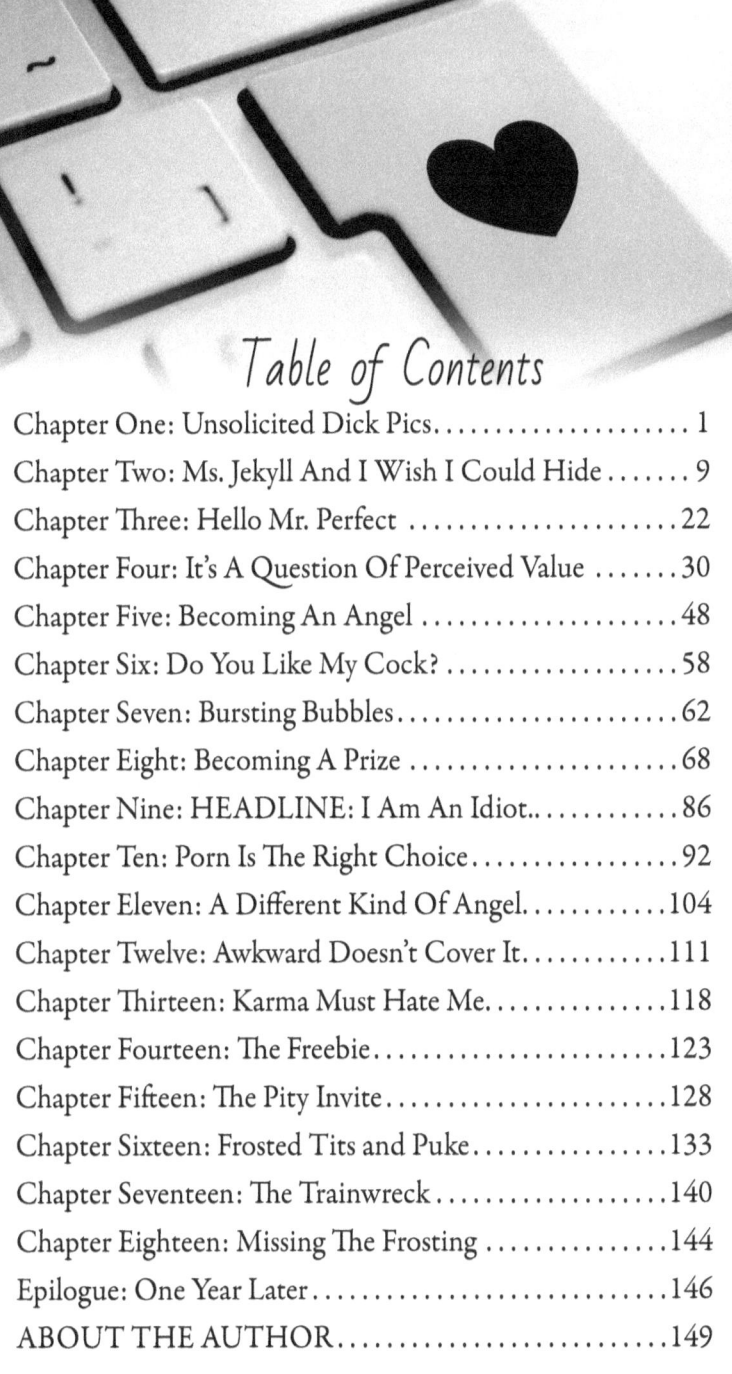

Table of Contents

Chapter One

Unsolicited Dick Pics

Chrissy

"Why did a picture of a penis just appear on your phone?" The tone of Raquel's voice told me she was not only shocked, but also judging me.

I sighed, grabbed the phone off the table, and clicked on the text to see who sent it. It was Sean #3.

"It's nobody," I managed to say without sighing too much and putting the phone face down on the table just in case Sean #3 felt the need to share from a different angle.

"So, you have random strangers sending you pictures of their dicks?" Now the judgment had escalated and wasn't subtle.

Raquel was one of those friends you have that is in the "perfect" relationship. She met her now fiancé in college, freshman year. They fell in love on their first date and wore matching sweaters to holiday parties and had couple Halloween costumes. Basically, they are the kind of couple you hate when you are single and lonely.

Raquel was staring at me over her pumpkin spice latte with her arms crossed, waiting for an answer. I didn't want to give one. I was ridiculously tired of explaining myself to her. Which I felt happened each and every time we were together.

Raquel was the most "maintained" friend I have. I use the word maintained because Raquel—never call her Rachel by the way—never had a hair out of place, always had flawless make-up, and inevitably wore amazing and perfectly fitted clothes.

I, on the other hand, seemed to always come across as a hippy art student. I am a hippy art student, or more specifically, I was one. It has been three years since I graduated with a Masters in Art History from Columbia University.

The last argument in regard to dating was about how I did not believe that dating sites could correctly match anyone with stupid questions like "Do you prefer coffee or tea?" Who the hell cares? This isn't, usually, a reason not to date someone. Also, the percentage match ratings were usually off base. Of course, we had this argument partially because I had never matched with someone above 50%.

Raquel cleared her throat to get my attention. This was not simply going to go away.

I took another swig of my latte and tried my best to look her in the face. "It is from a guy that I went on a date with...once." I didn't know why I felt compelled to explain myself "Obviously, it didn't work out." But I always did with her.

Her eyes narrowed, and she pursed her lips before saying, "Obviously."

I wasn't sure what was actually worse in this situation. The fact that Sean #3 had been one of the better dates on the list of the bad dates that I had been on recently, or that there was such a lengthy list of bad dates to choose from.

Raquel decided to change subjects to how it was going at work. We both worked at the same law firm in New York City. Raquel was a legal aid. I was a legal typist. My degree landed me a typist job. My parents were not very impressed since they had paid for my education. They had both believed I was getting a degree in Business with a minor in Art History. Instead, I had received a degree in Art History with a minor in Philosophy. It was an impressive education for a being a professor, running a gallery, or working at a museum. None of these jobs ever actually became available in New York, and if by some miracle they did, the job would go to someone with actual experience. I did not have experience.

"Did you ever end up going out with Mitchell?" Raquel asked after gossiping about several of our co-workers. Another one of the great characteristics of my friend Raquel is she loves to gossip. I would like to say we are both better people but we're not.

"Not exactly" was my reply. The subject of Mitchell was another one of those doors I did not intend on opening with her.

"What does that mean?" Either Raquel couldn't take a hint or my hints were so subtle that they were impossible for anyone to pick up on. My fear is the latter.

"It means that I wouldn't consider what happened between us 'going out' exactly." I made quotations with my fingers when I said those words.

I had a choice in this moment: I could continue with my explanation or make her pull it out of me. I decided to make her work for it.

There is something that I truly know about myself: I was never one of those people that can rip a bandage right off. I would rather wait for it to fall off instead of causing myself any pain.

"What would you consider it then?" Although Raquel was in the perfect romantic relationship, she was a very hard person to be friends with at times like this.

"I would consider it a brief meeting" was my reply. I could tell my unwillingness to give all the details was driving her a little nuts. It was nice to see the expression when this happened. It meant I was sorta winning. Pathetic, I know.

"A meeting?" she asked. "What kind of 'meeting?'" She used air quotes this time.

I shrugged. "The kind of meeting that involves him fucking me in the copier room at work."

This created the desired effect of Raquel's eyes becoming quite large and "WHAT?" issued forth from her mouth at a volume that caused most of the patrons of the coffee shop to turn their heads.

I took another sip of my latte.

"Are you fucking kidding me?" she lowered her voice about mid-sentence. "At work? Are you crazy?"

This line of questioning continued for a couple of minutes. As usual, I simply let it. It was not fruitful to answer these questions until she had uttered every single one that had come to mind. Then it was best to choose the ones you felt safe answering.

As far as it being at 'Work,' it was widely known at Claremont, Fitzman, Waterton, Marcalls, Smith, Venderstand, Hallston, Shadearn, Mickleton, Gorden, Collins-Marks, Tracer, & Butterton: Attorneys at Law (aka Work) that you were: a) not to sleep with fellow co-workers as this can create an uncomfortable work environment and b) definitely not supposed to do it while at work.

The final question arrived, "So, was it any good?" and I decided it was somewhat safe to answer.

Mitchell had only been at the firm for about a year. He had graduated at the top of his class and was an up and coming corporate merger lawyer.

In order to succeed at any law firm, you basically have to give up almost your entire life to do it. It has to become what you do until you break through and then only most of your life is consumed until you make partner. This isn't even getting your name listed on the business cards.

I, on the other hand, had to work a lot of overtime to cover the rent for the room I rented from a cousin. I was lucky; I lived in a five story walk-up about seven blocks from Times Square. It was "rent controlled" and my aunt had been on the city board so when places became available, the family of the board members found out about them first. It is very mafia-like without all the murders and money laundering.

I decided to just simply tell Raquel the entire story of what happened with the amazing Mitchell, or Mitch which is what he asked me to call him; it just seemed easier this way.

The Mitch Encounter which I would later dub it occurred about two weeks ago. It had been a Thursday night and there were only a couple of us still at the office around 10pm. I was sitting in one of the rooms full of cubicles where they kept the typists. They had a fancier name for us which was "Administrative Specialists" which was intended to make us feel as if we are an important part of the team. Unfortunately, since the only people that knew our names were the other specialists sitting in the cubes next to us, it was just a title we ended up explaining when a person asked what we did for a living.

I had my headphones in, and I was listening to a playlist I had created of my favorite songs that I loved to sing every time I heard them. They kept me motivated to not get depressed when I thought about the fact that I was not doing what I love; instead, I was doing the work I needed to pay the bills.

I suddenly felt someone tap on my shoulder, and it caused me to jump.

"Hey. Sorry. I didn't mean to scare you." It was Mitchell, err Mitch.

Mitch was about 5'10". He had brown hair he kept fairly short but still a little more stylish than most of the suits in the office. His eyes were a caramel brown, and he had the nice build of someone who plays a sport with his friends in his spare time.

I pulled out the headphones and said, "Hi."

Mitchell smiled at me and asked, "What are you doing?"

I blushed a little. "Working on the Dawson case." If I wasn't so thrown off by the fact that a cute, young, successful man was talking to me, it would have occurred to me that he knew exactly what I was doing.

He leaned in to the cubicle. "So how late are you staying?"

"Umm... I don't know... why?" I asked, trying to seem coy.

He leaned in a little closer and ran his hand along my arm. "I was thinking maybe we could get a drink." He was so close that I could smell his cologne and the slight smell of the energy drinks I had seen him constantly walking around with.

I was sure in that moment that I smelled like coffee and hoped in the same moment I didn't smell at all like the tuna sandwich I had for lunch.

"Sure... I mean... that would be great." I was listening to myself sound like a complete idiot.

He nodded his head in the direction of the door. I smiled. Saved the file I was working on, clocked myself out, and grabbed my purse.

We headed to a bar around the corner. Mitchell insisted on two things after the first beer. First, that I call him Mitch, and second, that we should be doing some shots: six to be exact. It was all just fun, right?

Needless to say, I am a lightweight. At some point during the laughing and the flirting, Mitch slid his hand up my thigh. I froze, even being in my state of intoxication, I was not sure what to do in situations like this. He then leaned in and kissed me. The kind of kiss where you feel his hand in your hair, smashing his face into yours. It was hot.

It was a few minutes later that Mitch convinced me that neither of us was in a condition to drive, and we should head back to the office to "sober up" a little.

We ended up in the copier room because it was one of the few rooms without cameras.

Mitch had convinced the drunk me that he had "always fantasized about me" and that I was "so fucking sexy." This was enough to allow him to slide my skirt up, my panties down, and to take me from behind while I leaned over the color copier in the back corner. At the time, it seemed so passionate and amazing.

When he finished—not we, but he—he removed the condom and tied it, putting it in his pocket. He said he would walk me out but only made it as far as the elevator before he "remembered" something he had to wrap up. He said he looked forward to seeing me tomorrow and hopefully would take me out on a real date soon. He kissed me on the cheek. I took a cab home. I was afraid I would fall asleep on the subway.

I woke up the next morning still with the silly idea that Mitch and I were starting something real. Even some of the romance novels I have read had a cute premise like this. It can happen after all.

Then I arrived at work.

As fate would have it, Mitch arrived at the exact same time as I did. I was in the elevator, and he jumped in as the doors were closing. He took one look at me and instead of returning my smile, he turned his back to me. The moment it dinged on our floor, he almost pushed the doors off to get out of the elevator.

I spent most of the day thinking of what it could all mean. Was he behaving this way because we were at work? Was he worried our relationship would create issues?

Yes, that was me, overanalyzing the entire thing and on top of that, reading into our late night fuck that we had a relationship of some kind.

It actually took me a full week to realize I was a quick lay for him. That instead of actually being interested in me at all, he was interested in what 2-for-1 shots could get him. Which apparently was me bent over a copier.

I could tell that at the end of this story there were so many things crossing Raquel's mind right now. I took another long sip of my latte. The story sounded even more pathetic when I said it out loud.

"Did you get tested?" she finally asked.

"Tested?" I replied.

"Yes. Tested. You need to make sure he didn't give you anything, you know, like herpes." She shook her head as if she just tasted something incredibly sour.

"He wore a condom."

"That doesn't mean anything. I read an article just the other day where a woman got AIDS and her partner wore a condom. They are not 100%, you know. You need to go get a test so you don't spread anything he gave you. You haven't slept with anyone else, have you? If you did, you will have to tell him. Oh my god! I would be so embarrassed..." I tuned her out again.

Although I would like to think Raquel wouldn't actually affect me, I was, of course, wrong. It took three days for her words to finally drive me into a worried frenzy, so I went down to the free clinic and got tested... for everything.

I got a voicemail from the clinic that the only thing I had was a yeast infection. This, I suppose, was the good news. You can easily treat a yeast infection.

Texting Raquel to tell her I didn't have one of the "venereal gifts that keeps on giving" was the bad news. She had talked to the girls in her part of the office, and they all said Mitchell was a player. He had slept his way through more than half the women at work. Yep, this day just kept getting better and better.

Ms. Jekyll And I Wish I Could Hide

SCHUYLER

I sat at the computer, blinds closed, pants down around my ankles, a chair in front of my bedroom door, keying in the URL with my left hand. I only had to type the first five letters and the full address auto-populated. Jekyll's smiling face appeared immediately.

"Hi, Schuyler."

I tried to look happy. "Hi, Jekyll."

"Good to see you again."

"You, too."

"How are you?"

"Oh. You know."

She cocked an eyebrow flirtatiously. "*Do* I?"

"You know better than anybody."

"I don't believe that."

"Believe it."

"OK, well, then I say you're fine."

"All right."

"What does 'all right' mean?"

"It means fine."

"Does that mean you're fine?"

"It means I'm . . . as fine as I ever am, I guess. How are *you*?"

"I'm good," she said with the faintest air of exasperation, then abruptly brightened and changed the subject. "Hey! I have something to show you."

"Really? What is it?"

"Look what my friend got for me." She reached out of the frame and picked up a cake, which she held up in front of the Webcam lens.

"Ooohhh! That's a nice cake. What's the occasion?"

"She made it for my dissertation defense."

"It's beautiful."

"It is, isn't it?"

"So tell me about your dissertation defense."

"I'm arguing that the Smoot-Hawley Tariff, although it was not one of the main causes of the Great Depression—because foreign trade was only a small sector of the U.S. economy at the time, you see—nonetheless was a major contributing factor leading to the rise of Imperial Japan's campaign of aggressive expansionist colonialism."

"Wow," I said, stroking myself. "That sounds *very* interesting."

"Thank you. I hope the committee agrees."

"Have you been working on it long?"

"Yes, a couple of years now."

"What got you interested in that?"

"I read a book about the history of the Far East and the author argued that it was largely U.S. fiscal policy that led to war in the Pacific."

"Wow, really?" I stroked myself with increasing vigor.

"Not to imply exclusive causality."

"No, of course not."

"But it *was* highly emblematic of the type of economic isolationist ideology that pushed the island to feel compelled to pursue an agenda of pan-Asian heg . . ." Jekyll frowned and scrunched her nose. "Heg . . . Heg-ee?" She fumbled and bit her lip. "Heg-ee-mon? I'm sorry. I don't—"

"*Hegemony*," I prompted. "You know, like, regional dominance?"

"Right, right, yeah. I'm so sorry."

"Don't apologize."

"OK."

"Keep going. You're doing great."

"Anyway, I'm defending it tomorrow, so I've been challenging myself with every possible line of rhetorical attack I can imagine." (She pronounced it *rhuh-het-o-RICK-al*, but I let it go.)

"Are you saving the cake for after it's over? Your defense, I mean?"

"Oh, yes! It's a very, very special cake."

"Are you afraid you might spoil it?"

"Yes," she said, making a sad face. "I'd hate to ruin such a beautiful cake. I'd feel terrible if anything happened to it."

"Yes." I nodded slowly. "You would feel so guilty, wouldn't you, to mess up something that somebody spent so much time and effort to get just right for you."

Jekyll adjusted her giant round glasses. "Do you mind if I take my hair down, Schuyler?"

"No, no. Of course not. Not at all. Please, make yourself totally comfortable. Just pretend that I'm not even here."

She reached around behind her head and slid out the #2 Dixon Ticonderoga that held her top bun in place. She shook out her dark brown mass of shiny, loose curls. They fell past her shoulders. Running her fingers through them to add volume, she grinned at me. I stroked harder.

"It's so hot in here, Schuyler."

"You can unbutton your shirt, if you want."

"You wouldn't mind?"

"I wouldn't mind at all."

"I don't want you to think I'm being a tease, or anything."

"No, no, that's perfectly fine. You do whatever makes you feel comfortable."

She opened the front of her shirt, button by button. "I feel a little self-conscious doing this in front of you."

"Don't be shy. We're friends, right? We should be relaxed around our friends."

"I feel *very* relaxed around you, Schuyler." She slipped her shirt off, revealing a pink underwire balconette bra with cups one size too small. The reinforced panels, clearly designed by the U.S. Department of Defense using advanced strategic materials, somehow supported (and barely contained) her huge breasts. Bulging rolls of flawless white flesh escaped from the thin and mostly translucent membrane of delicate floral lace. It was an undergarment on the verge of explosion. The visual effect was stunning, evocative of a pair of five-pound Jell-O molds balanced precariously on a narrow mantelpiece.

She made a small gesture of modesty, as flimsy and false as the coverage afforded by that wonderfully wispy film of a bra, holding up a hand generally in front of her, not enough to actually cover anything or block my view in any meaningful way, in the same fashion that a person breaks into a kind of stylized jogging motion when he realizes he is in someone's way, without actually going any faster. "I hope you don't think I'm a dirty girl for taking off my clothes in front of you, Schuyler." As she spoke, she moved her upper body much more than necessary, rotating her shoulders expertly to induce a variety of bouncing and jiggling motions. A pair of monumental protuberances bulged emphatically through the lace, as turgid as I was. If her areolae were Venn diagrams of the girls I found physically attractive, her jutting nipples were the subset of girls who knew how to say all the right things.

"It doesn't bother me."

"I don't want you to get the wrong idea about me, Schuyler."

"Not at all, not at all."

"You just make me feel so at ease with myself. You know? I feel like I can be totally . . . *natural* around you."

"Good, I'm glad. I'm very glad."

"This cake is so pretty."

"*You're* pretty."

"Oh, stop. You're making me blush."

"Your friend must care a lot about you, to make a cake like that."

"She does. She's very proud of me."

"Is she proud of your accomplishments?"

"She's *very* proud of my accomplishments."

"Does that cake mean a lot to you?"

"It means *so* much to me. You have no idea. It means so. Much." She leaned forward. Her breasts dipped into the icing, leaving two small but distinct divots. "Oh, *no*!"

"What did you do?"

She twisted her face into a sorrowful pout. "I screwed up the cake, Schuyler."

"How did you screw it up?"

"With my tits. I screwed it up with my tits. Oh, look! It's all over me! What a mess."

"It's all over your bra."

"Oh my god, you're totally right. I guess I should probably take it off." She glanced around, as if we were in a public place. "But . . . I probably shouldn't do that in front of you."

"I don't mind."

"Really?"

"No, I don't mind at all."

"It wouldn't bother you, if I took my bra off, right here in front of you like this?"

"No. Not a bit. Not even a little bit. You do whatever you need to do. It's fine."

She suppressed a coy giggle that caused tremors across her spectacular rack. "You wouldn't think I'm an awful person?"

"I would never think that."

"Wow, you're so sweet."

"Well, we're friends, right? Friends should feel at ease around each other. Friends shouldn't ever make friends feel uptight or uncomfortable."

"OK, then. If you don't mind." She turned around so that her back was to the camera. She unhooked each of the four clasps, one at a time. Then she turned back around to face me. She smiled innocently. She shrugged off the straps, then lowered the cups. Those boobs, sweet holy Jesus those magnificent boobs, they came spilling out, still imprinted with the pink lines where the edges dug into her skin. Her left areola was more oval than circular, bumpy and puckered. Her right one was smoother, rounder, and wider, positioned higher on her breast, delimited by a single green vein. My eyes darted back and forth between them as she leaned forward again.

"Oh no," she exclaimed.

"What is it?"

"I screwed up the cake some more. And look, Schuyler! I got icing all over my tits!"

"That's terrible," I said.

"You know what, though?"

"What? Tell me."

"I have to admit: it feels kind of good."

"The icing on your tits?"

"Yes, the icing on my tits. It feels good."

"You like the way that feels?"

"I do. I do like the way it feels."

"Well, since the cake is screwed up anyway," I pointed out, "you may as well get some more icing on them."

"I suppose I may as well," she agreed. "After all, it feels so good when I do . . . *this*." She dipped her finger into the top of the cake and excavated a trench, extracting an extravagant quantity of the sticky, sugary, fluffy stuff, which she then proceeded to smear all over her cleavage with wanton abandon.

Every muscle in my body tensed, I hunched over with an involuntary series of spastic convulsions, and I made an expression like I was giving birth to a riveted aluminum octahedron while a pair of dryads sucked on my toes.

"How was that?" she asked when I was done.

"Good," I replied breathlessly. "It was good. Real good. Thank you." I reached for a tissue. I had to use my left hand to hold my hairy, blubbery, and slightly sweaty belly up out of the way so I could see what I was doing while I dabbed ejaculate off the chair, the bottom of the desk, my inner thigh and a patch of the stained, worn-out carpet.

"Are we all done?" She winked at me.

"Yeah. Yeah."

"OK. I'll see you on Wednesday," she said, blowing me a kiss. "Bye!" Then the feed went blank. The screen flashed: $38.36. A significant chunk of my weekly take-home pay. Worth every penny.

Finishing my familiar post-onanism cleanup ritual, I half-stood as I tugged my boxers and jeans back up into place. I looked in the mirror, straightened my T-shirt, and adjusted my glasses. I needed to shave. I could use a haircut, too. Feathery, oily waves of hair the color of tree bark stuck out at crooked and incongruous angles over my ears and behind my neck. It wasn't even a good kind of brown. It was a greasy, dull kind of brown, like compost or fingernail dirt. Like last week's rejected brownies. Like the skin on bean soup.

I sat on the edge of the bed. The digital clock on the bedside stand displayed a series of red LED bars, some blinking or flickering, but not enough of them to form readable numerals. I opened the drawer and took out her picture. I looked at it for a long time.

I wanted to stay in my room, but I was hungry. I could hear them out there, and the urge to hide right there where I was tempted me to ignore my craving for carbs. I put her picture away and reached for a Terry Pratchett book instead. Flopping down on the ancient, smelly, germ-infested mattress that was somehow still supported by the groaning, creaking, sagging bedframe underneath it, I tried to read. For a few minutes, it worked. But my stomach's persistent rumbling soon overbalanced my pathological aversion to my fellow apartment dwellers, so with a sigh I set Discworld aside and got up. I took a deep breath and opened the door.

Fuck, *all* of them were home: Paranoid Roommate, Idiot Roommate, and Mean Roommate. I was afraid of that. The trouble with living in New York is you can't do it alone.

Paranoid Roommate designs databases and gets paid quite well to do it. He is absolutely convinced of three things:

The U.S. government, the insurance companies, the petroleum industry, and the military are in control of everything. EVERYTHING. When the store is out of his brand of orange juice, it's part of a conspiracy.

He is being watched at all times, his movements monitored, his actions studied. This is because since he "knows what's really going on," he is a "threat" to the "system." (As opposed to a "moron" with no "clue.")

A total meltdown of civilization is imminent. It will involve violent revolution, panic in the streets, the imposition of martial law, forced-labor camps, violent clashes with federal troops, food shortages, and the collapse of the Internet and the global power grid.

He is getting ready for all of these things by making careful and thorough preparations. And by "making careful and thorough preparations," I mean blogging, playing video games, smoking a lot of weed, and talking to his paranoid friends about how they are going to create their own independent, self-sufficient society.

The simple fact is, none of them would have any idea how to grow tomatoes, build a house, or install a solar panel, let alone hunt deer with a bow and arrow, or whatever the fuck they think they're going to do. They're all software engineers and network security admins.

He mumbles endlessly about his vague plans for a device that extracts unlimited energy from the Earth's magnetic field and how he's been "studying" ancient Eastern bare-handed combat techniques so that he can defend himself and escape into the hills when the need arises. Listening to him is sort of like listening to A.M. radio talk shows, only less entertaining.

Idiot Roommate is, quite literally, the dumbest human being alive. You might think that's a hyperbole, but I challenge you to prove otherwise. Other people might have lower IQs, but they are generally strapped down to the bed, drooling on themselves. A lobotomized hamster could outwit Idiot Roommate, if it came down to that. I'd pay to see that fight.

There are few things in this world more profoundly annoying than a dumb person who thinks of himself as smart and freely shares his opinions and his understanding of "facts" with everyone as if he's doing them a huge favor. He does it with a smug look that clearly implies he thinks we're lucky to be blessed with his superior insights and charming personality.

Meanwhile, in reality, he can't even spell his own name. He can hardly put two coherent sentences together in conversation. Yet in his mind, somehow he is erudite and articulate, his logic irrefutable, his wisdom unquestionable. You know how an anorexic girl can see her scrawny, emaciated body in the mirror, bones sticking out all over the place, and see herself as fat? Idiot Roommate is like that. He can say something preposterously stupid and incomprehensible, and he hears his own utterance as marvelously brilliant, the gilded oratory of a polymath genius.

His vocabulary is, to say the least, limited, but unfortunately he doesn't ever say the least. He has a cozy little arsenal of words to deploy, and he doesn't even use them correctly most of the time. He makes random word substitutions, which is like using salt instead of sugar in a recipe because, hey, they're both white and granular. Recently he said, "stucco" when he meant, "staccato." Another time I recall he said New York City was "polarizing" and I'm pretty sure he was trying to say it was getting to be cold. He also seems to think "stealthy" means "odious"—which sort of makes sense, I guess, since it's like a cross between "smelly," "stinky" and "filthy." Still, words don't always mean what they sound like. That's just not how words work. But you can't convince him he's wrong about anything; he's stubborn as a particularly dense and unusually slow-moving boulder. He also has a very short memory, however, and next week he's likely to be telling YOU the same thing you spent an hour trying to no avail to convince HIM was true.

He believes he wins every conversation. (Conversations aren't something you have. They are something you win or lose.) He also believes that people are afraid to engage him in debate for this reason. And finally, he feels a moral obligation to patiently "explain" to everyone why he or she is wrong about whatever they're doing or talking about.

Idiot Roommate works as a clerk at a music store. He thinks of himself as being "outside the System"—I'm sure he would spell it with a capital S if he knew how capitalization worked and what it was for—and he's proud of the way he isn't "trapped" by having a conventional "conformist" job. Believe it or not, he has a Bachelor's degree in Humanities. He was a C and D student in an age where even mediocre academic skills at a third-rate community college will get you a B, and he'll gladly tell you that it was because school "bored" him. It just wasn't enough to stimulate his staggering creative intellect. His parents paid for his education. He works just enough to pay his share of the rent and buy junk food. He spends all the rest of his time on his one and only hobby, which is trolling the Internet criticizing everyone, and getting into prolonged arguments on forums and in chatrooms.

And then there's Mean Roommate. Mean Roommate gets paid to be mean. He sort of reminds me of the sadistic dentist from *Little Shop of Horrors*.

He gets paid a *lot* to be mean, which I take as final proof that God does not exist. Either that or He's more of an Old Testament God, the kind that shrugs and says things like, "eh, what do you expect? Fair, you want things to be? Have you been paying attention? Look around. Tell me, what's fair? Go eat a sandwich. Watch some TV. Leave me alone."

During the day, he works at a collection agency. (Mean Roommate, not God.) He makes a very nice salary harassing people who are facing the worst times in their lives: bankruptcy, death, debt, divorce, unemployment, prolonged illness, defaulting on student loans etc.

No one wants that job because no one likes being a bully or a jerk eight hours a day. Except Mean Roommate. He *loves* it. Sucking at the teat of the law of supply and demand, extending the invisible middle finger of Adam Smith to the world, he gets paid an inordinate sum to be a rare asshole. He comes home and crows proudly about all the "dumb twats" he deals with, while Idiot Roommate nods sympathetically. He always seems to think it's their fault. Sometimes it probably is, I guess, or at least partly, but he takes such delight in stomping on people who are already crawling in the mud, their lives in shambles. He tells us these heartbreaking stories, and he just laughs and laughs.

Three nights a week, he works as a bouncer at a club five blocks from our apartment. It's a terrible place. The cops and/or the paramedics get called over there almost every week, sometimes twice in one night. Gunfights in the parking lot are common. He loves it. He doesn't get paid much; he just really enjoys beating the ever-loving shit out of people for little or no reason. Funny story: he used to work at a nice club where there was never any trouble, and he hated it. He was bored. He never got to punch anyone in the face.

He's a bodybuilder, and he takes enough steroids to hobble a yak. He sucks down those 5-Hour Energy® shots all day long and snorts coke when he can get it. He spent a few years studying mixed martial arts, but now all he does is go to the gym. He's the size of a truck.

The weird thing is, despite the fact that he is an absolute irredeemable thoroughbred scumwad and a cruel, violent prick, he has three girlfriends. And he cheats on all of them with other girls. I don't even know what his total girl-count is.

He's always telling all of them how fat and ugly they are. He tells them they have chunky thighs and saggy asses and flat chests and stupid hair. He tells them to wear more makeup because they look like shit. He tells them their clothes are ridiculous. He makes fun of everything they say and do.

And they can't get enough of it. All three of them are always crying and apologizing to him and promising to try harder and be prettier and nicer for him. Whenever one of them confronts him about fucking around all over the place, it always ends with him calling her frigid and/or a filthy disgusting slut (sometimes both in the course of the same argument) and threatening to dump her, and she starts sobbing and begging him not to go and telling him how sorry she is. They give him money, too.

Living with him is basically a nightmare except for one thing: when he calls the landlord, SHIT GETS FIXED.

So you can understand why I made my way as quietly and unobtrusively to the kitchen as possible. I would do anything to avoid calling attention to myself. I wore only my socks. (The floor was gross, but then again so were my socks.) I opened the fridge. As usual, it was mostly filled with takeout food that had spoiled during the previous presidential administration. I pulled out a crusty, mostly empty jar of off-brand spaghetti sauce and set it on the countertop. I rummaged around in the cabinets until I found a packet of egg noodles. There were ants all over the outside, and a few on the inside too, but I shook or flicked most of them off. I found a saucepan in the sink that was kind of clean, wiped it out with a damp paper towel and rotated the faucet knob. Running hot water in our apartment causes the walls to make alternating moaning and hammering sound. Running the cold water produces a high, shrill whine. I looked out the tiny window, past the dead plants on the fire escape, at the graffiti-adorned brick wall on the other side of the alley, about ten feet away. I turned on the right front burner, the only part of the stove that worked. A scurrying motion caught my eye, and I looked down in time to see a gray mouse disappearing into a gap between the mildewed vinyl flooring and the crumbling drywall. Behind me, I could hear Mean Roommate snorting about some dumb goddamn faggot whose bullshit he had to put up with today, while Paranoid Roommate played *World of Warcraft* and rambled about something to do with FEMA camps. Idiot Roommate was experimenting with sticking marbles up his nose. I tried to focus my attention outside the window. A pigeon flew by and took a shit.

CHAPTER THREE

Hello Mr. Perfect

CHRISSY

The time I actually had that wasn't absorbed with work, laundry, eating or sleeping, I spent at museums or gallery shows. Since I was still waiting for my big break, I felt it was important to be a part of the community. I, of course knew all the classics, but knowing the up and coming artists was key to getting a job in this industry.

I had two little black dresses that I would alternate between shows. I made sure to use different pieces to accessorize, but I knew I couldn't compete with the socialites that I saw regularly at these events. There is a hierarchy in the art community. Unfortunately, you are not an artist truly unless a person who has the clout tells you that you are or "discovers you."

This was the ugly part of the industry. You could be amazing, but it didn't matter unless someone who can't paint a help wanted sign tells the world that it should care.

Tonight's show was at a gallery called "The End." It was in an up and coming part of the city. The gallery was featuring a neo-realist painter named simply Ben.

I am not a huge fan of neo-realist work, but again, that isn't why I was there. I grabbed a glass of champagne and began to make my rounds, both studying the work and seeing who, of the who's-who, was in attendance.

As I wandered, I noticed several socialites, but they only really spoke with other people they thought were important, namely themselves. There were a few gallery owners in attendance; I re-introduced myself by knowing who they were and telling them that their gallery was "stunning" or "breathtaking." They would smile and thank me for taking an interest. They would all ask me if I knew the artist. I didn't, of course. I found that telling them I had a passion for art and that I was simply a huge fan was the best approach. The times I tried to mention my degree simply ended in them getting fairly uncomfortable and waiting for me to walk away, or a couple times they did just walk away without making an excuse as to why.

I was waiting to speak with Susan Stragalli of the Trinity Gallery, who was speaking with a socialite wearing a pair of $5,000 shoes when I felt someone stand next to me.

"Aren't you supposed to be staring at the paintings and not gallery owners?" said a deep masculine voice. I felt my cheeks begin to get flushed. I turned to look at my new observer and found a set of amazingly deep blue eyes staring back at me.

"Kevin," he said and reached out his hand.

"Christina," I replied and took his hand in mine. This of course required me to change the hand my glass of champagne was in and being the "graceful" person that I am I ended up spilling it right down the top of my dress.

I began to wonder if I was simply cursed.

I was trying to assess the damage on my dress and at the same time I was also looking around with the hope that the yelp I made had not made too big of a scene.

Only a couple people had apparently heard and were watching me now with condescending looks as if whatever conversation I had interrupted was an important discussion on world peace. My stomach sank as I realized Susan was one of those people.

"Are you ok?" Kevin's voice cut through the range of not-so-positive emotions I was experiencing.

"I'm... I'm... Wet" was what decided to spill from my lips at that moment.

He laughed. It was a deep, warm, sexy laugh that I found caused me to get goosebumps.

I stood there with no earthly idea of what to do at this moment. Here was a gorgeous, seemingly successful guy, based on his suit and shoes, flirting with me, and I sounded like an idiot. What else is new?

"So, are you an artist?" I knew he wasn't. Even the question escaping my lips with the higher pitch at the end indicated I knew the answer.

"No, I am a collector..." he started, again holding my gaze with those deep blue eyes "...of things that I find beautiful."

I couldn't believe this was happening. I have watched a thousand romantic movies with lines like this. It was exhilarating. I had to pull it together.

Without losing his gaze, I smiled. "Have you found anything you want to collect tonight?"

I agree this was not the best line. It also was not the worst line that I could have said either.

He smiled, and his fingers moved to tuck a loose curl behind my ear. His touch sent shivers through my entire body. I felt my face flush again. There was no hiding from him the effect he had on me.

His tongue wet his lips as he let his eyes wander the length of me and then back up, "Yes. I believe I have."

My knees felt as if they were going to buckle.

"Can I give you a ride?" he asked and before he got the last word out of his mouth I said "YES!" He smiled again. I was happy he found my desperation cute at this point.

He gestured towards the door and placed his hand gently on my lower back to guide me out.

Was I doing this? My head was spinning. *I was doing this!* I wanted to text Raquel and tell her what was happening. It was surreal. I didn't. Text her that is. It would have been rude, and although I was buzzed, I had enough common sense to know that wouldn't be taken well.

When we arrived outside, there was, in fact, a car waiting. The driver opened the door and Kevin let me slide into the backseat of the town car and then sat next to me.

The driver closed the door and Kevin moved his arm up so it was resting on the top of the seat and his fingers began to play with the back of my neck. This sent shivers down my spine.

"Where do you live?" he asked. I said the cross streets and the car started to move. "So, are you married? Boyfriend?" his voice was so much deeper it seemed now that we were in such a confined space. I shook my head. My throat was suddenly dry. I licked my lips. His eyes moved to watch my action. It was almost as if he was studying me.

"You are beautiful, Christina." He said this as he leaned in closer. I was going to orgasm right there. No man had ever spoken to me like this. His lips were so close that I could feel his hot breath against my face. He just hovered there for a moment as we stared into each other's eyes. Then he pressed his lips against mine, so gentle at first, and I closed my eyes.

His kiss became more urgent. He felt his tongue slide between my lips and a small noise escaped me as I felt my core tingle. My arms moved around his shoulders, and I brought myself closer to him. As our mouths explored each other, I couldn't get enough. I lost myself in the moment. He tasted like red wine, and every noise I made caused his intensity to increase. He was devouring me.

I hadn't even realized the car had arrived at my apartment until the driver cleared his throat caused me to break the connection with Kevin. Which I instantly missed.

Kevin's lips were pink and swollen only as making out can do. I wanted to launch myself into him again. Instead, he opened the door and got out, holding his hand out to me to help me out. It was over and too soon.

I tried to not have the disappointment show on my face. Did I try to get his number? Should I offer mine? So many things raced through my mind as I stood and made sure my dress was pulled down in all the right places.

"You are amazing." He was smiling. "I would like to see you again. How does picking you up on Tuesday at eight sound?" His voice was so husky I felt something tighten between my thighs.

"I'll be ready," I said, smiling back.

He leaned in kissing me again gently on the lips "It's a date." And he got in his town car, and it pulled away with me still watching.

I spun around and stared up at the sky. This was possibly the best night I had ever had.

I ran upstairs as quickly as I could. Once inside, I made sure to relock all the doors. No matter how elated I was, I lived in the city and safety needed to be first. The irony of making out with a complete stranger of course eluded me at that moment.

I went into my bedroom, closed the door, and unzipped the dress, letting it fall to the floor. I climbed onto the bed, laying on my back I ran my fingers across my still swollen lips. Closing my eyes, I let my fingers wander down my chest, down my stomach, and across my black lace panties.

I had on a matching set, not because anything like this had ever happened at one of these events, or my life. I wore matching bra and panties because it made me feel a little more sophisticated. Right now the sophistication between my legs was soaking wet.

I slid my fingers under the fabric and began to move them between my moist folds. I closed my eyes and imagined Kevin's mouth between my legs. I imagined his tongue running the length of me, tasting me. I could imagine the feel of his lips as he sucked on my clit. My fingers mimicking what he would do to me. I came hard. I pulled a pillow over my face so I wasn't too loud. I would hate for my cousin to hear me. Namely because I didn't want to answer any questions.

I waited until the morning to text Raquel. I told her I had met a tall dark handsome stranger with his own town car at a gallery. She was, of course, intrigued. We stole away at break to walk to the Starbucks across the street to grab some coffee. She grilled me the entire way and although in my mind it was the most amazingly romantic moment of my life, Raquel thought I was crazy.

I think this was mostly spurred on by the fact that no matter what question she asked me, I didn't have an answer. I knew the following things: his name was Kevin, what he looked like, he had a town car or at least drove in one, and he was picking me up Tuesday to do something.

By the end of break, and fifteen minutes with Raquel, I felt as if I was an idiot for enjoying any of it. She pointed out that now some guy that I didn't have ANY details on knew where I lived and my name, and I had practically thrown my clothes off on the first night we met.

Raquel's disapproving looks were enough to kill any high I was still on from the night before. Instead of having a cute, supporting conversation with my best girlfriend where she tells me she "can't wait to meet him," I ended up feeling like Tuesday night should be an episode of *To Catch a Predator.*

That night, while eating a pint of my favorite ice cream, I called my actual best friend in the entire universe: Jessica.

Jessica and I had met in middle school. Jessica had gone into teaching and quickly learned that she hated children. However, Jess had landed a very cushy job right out of college at a private school in upstate New York. This meant I didn't get to see her very often, due to both lack of time and lack of resources, mainly on my part.

"Heya babe, what's up?" her voice was immediately comforting. I asked at first how she was. I asked her how work was going. Even asked about her parents.

Jessica had also been dating a fellow teacher, which apparently the school frowned upon. It didn't help the situation that Jessica was a lesbian. We still live in a society that wants to be comfortable with freedoms, but at times, especially in a snooty private prep school in upstate New York, this would have been a double-no-no.

"So, how is..." I wanted to call her Brittney.

Jess laughed. "You mean Tiffany?"

"Yes. Tiffany. How are things?" I asked genuinely interested in at least that question.

"She is good. She quit." This is the exact type of response Jessica was great at. This is also why she is such a good teacher. She sucks you right in.

"Quit?" I had no choice but to ask.

"Yeah. She got tired of reading terrible essays from over-privileged, self-entitled rich kids. So, she decided to pursue her dream of writing full time."

"Wow!" I was stunned. Not just for Jessica, but for myself. What Tiffany had done was exactly what I thought of doing every day. However, I was too chicken-shit to do it.

"How is that going for her?" I was cringing, afraid of the answer. If she wasn't successful, then it would give more steam to my theory that I would never make it if I took the leap. If she was successful, then it would make me wallow. I shouldn't have even asked the question.

"Great, actually. She is an editor for two papers and has started her own group that brings authors together in various events. I has really taken off. The best part is I can take her on actual dates. No more sneaking around." Jessica sounded positively happy. This was good.

"So, Chris, why are you calling me? Not that I don't miss you, but you usually don't ask twenty-questions unless you have something on your mind." Jess knew.

With a small sigh, I began to tell her of the night, of Kevin, and what Raquel had said. I hoped my friend could see the movie ending side to this the way I had.

"I say go for it. Chris, you need happiness and possibly this is planet earth's way of finally giving that to you." As I listened to what she was saying, I finally released a breath I didn't even know I was holding.

"Thank you!" I exclaimed.

"Before you get too excited, make sure you keep track of where you are, and at least text me some details.... Just in case." She said the last part with the tone she uses when she knows she is saying something I don't want to hear.

"Agreed," I said.

We talked for a little while longer and came up with a plan. We decided that the best thing to do was no longer discuss this with Raquel. She had made me promise that I would not go out with Kevin or as she put it "whatever his real name is."

Jess and I hatched a plan. I would call in sick on Tuesday. That way I didn't have to explain anything, and I had a great alibi for where I would be all day. It was brilliant because Raquel was not the type of friend to bring soup and tissues by and my cousin hated her so I didn't have to worry about my roommate outing me. I felt like the James Bond of first dates.

Now to decide what to wear.

CHAPTER FOUR

It's A Question Of Perceived Value

SCHUYLER

Shay and I know each other from one of my horrible jobs. I have to specify that it's only one of them because I have three jobs, all of them horrible. I work a total of about 60 hours a week. Because those 60 hours are spread out over three different jobs, I get no overtime, but because I'm being paid under the table for two of them, I suppose I'm making back the difference in tax fraud.

Yeah, that's right, bitches. I just admitted to tax evasion right here in my own novel. That's what a smooth criminal I am. Totally badass motherfucker, right here. I will probably be turning away binders full of women lining up outside my apartment building holding up homemade posters offering to blow me for free. That's what you're dealing with.

I don't even care. I'm crazy or something generally along those lines. Fuck the police and all that. Stick it to the Man and what have you. I am, like, so totally dangerous and stuff. You can't handle it, because it's too real or something to that effect. Go ahead, Jack Lew, Secretary of the U.S. Treasury, tell the IRS to come and get me! I have already revealed enough details in this narrative that a cunning, by-the-book, old-school detective with a secret alcohol addiction related to guilt over the death of his wife at the hands of Chilean gangsters, when paired with a beautiful and brilliant but wise-cracking and rebellious red-headed, black-glasses-wearing forensic accountant on loan to the Agency from Scotland Yard could, after about a week of witty banter, unresolved sexual tension and slowly growing mutual respect, figure out exactly which street in New York I live on (it's a number), what apartment building I'm in (it rhymes with "coelacanth"), and even what color sneakers I'm wearing (blue). They would have to wait until Mean Roommate wasn't here to try to arrest me, because he would probably kill them both with his bare hands before they could put enough rounds in him to drop him. As soon as they busted in the door, Paranoid Roommate could probably take his cyanide suicide pill. (More likely he would just wet his pants.) I don't know what Idiot Roommate would do. Maybe he'd ask them what kinds of guns the government gives them, and are they allowed to shoot at birds and stuff, and do they get free jars of M&Ms since the government controls candy.

So then they'd haul me off to tax jail and calculate that I owe $439 for the past three years of undeclared income, plus a $50 fine. I would write them a check, which would bounce, because I haven't had more than $100 in the bank since I got a birthday check from my grandma in 2005 and she accidentally put in an extra zero. So then they'd probably get a court order to have me euthanized, since I clearly contribute nothing to society or the human race, and I'd think, well shit, they could have saved themselves a lot of trouble if they'd just shot me in the back of the head at the beginning, the way they did with Winston at the end of *1984*. I hope I'm not ruining the book for anyone. And what kind of name is Jack Lew, anyway?

Where was I? Oh yes, my three awful jobs.

My one and only legitimate job, as far as the city, county, state, and federal authorities know, is serving food at an inexplicably bad restaurant. New York City is known for its great food, and how this place can survive here is a mystery. Its clientele consists entirely of tourists, who never ever come back. We have no repeat business, which gives the servers a liberating sense of operating in a consequence-free environment. I would describe the food as Department of Health approved, but only just barely. The service is poor, yet slow, providing a counterpoint to the bad, overpriced food. It's an ideal place to eat for people who don't know how to check online reviews. All the servers hate each other. It's a diverse bunch of bitter losers: me and eight others. The other eight have nothing at all in common, and generally despise each other, but they are united in their hatred of me. They hate me more than they hate our boss, which is a lot. Our boss also hates me. I think the restaurant must be nothing more than a front for some sort of organized crime, maybe a syndicate that specializes in cheese-laundering or trafficking in substandard coleslaw. Maybe it will ultimately be the mob, and not the IRS, that shoots me in the back of the head. Oh well.

My second awful job is even more emotionally abusive. And it pays even less. I work for a guy who does local advertising. He's fairly tech-savvy, and he knows his way around Amazon and Goodreads, so I'm not going to go into any detail here other than to say it's a writing job—which is why I'm willing to put up with his daily flaming wagonloads of horseshit. The man is evil. He is a sadist, a bully, and a complete and total dick in every way. He enjoys nothing more than mocking me and my utter lack of talent and ability. Yet he doesn't fire me. In fact, he's been using my services for almost two years now. That in itself is almost an implied compliment. He does his best to negate it, however, with a never-ending stream of cruelty and malice. But at least I can say, honestly and accurately, that I am being paid to write. I am, technically speaking at least, a professional writer. I have no W-4, but someone is giving me cash in exchange for putting words together in a certain clever sequence, and that means a lot to me.

My third job is the worst of all. I work for a company that cleans out rental properties after they have been trashed. It's some of the most disgusting, degrading, and depressing work you can even imagine. Sometimes we find dead animals in there. Once one of my co-workers found a dead person. UNDER A BED. Yeah.

People often come to New York with their heads full of hopes and dreams. "If I can make it there," they sing badly and off-key, "I can make it anywhere." Then they actually get here and discover how dirty and noisy and expensive this town is, how unsympathetic, how brutal, how quick to trample you if you don't get moving or get out of the way. They end up sharing an apartment with as many room-mates as they can find. (At least I only have three, and at least our apartment is mostly structurally sound.) You'd be appalled at the conditions some people have to live in, right here in the middle of the biggest, richest city in America. A lot of them are immigrants, a lot of them are drug addicts, a lot of them have serious mental prob-lems, a lot of them are crooks, a lot of them are fleeing from terri-fying relationships, a lot of them are good kids who ran away from a suburban Midwestern life in search of excitement. But soon they find themselves in a damp, filthy hole with a dozen other people in a neighborhood like a war zone. The power gets turned off, the plumbing gets turned off, the Internet gets turned off (!) and until the day the cops show up to forcefully evict them, they're too broke and scared to leave.

That's when they bring us in to clean the place up. I'll let your imagination just run wild with that one. The only redeeming quality of that job is that it actually pays pretty well—better than the other two combined–but it's also irregular and unpredictable work. Most of my co-workers are ex-convicts. They all have the same story to tell. Bad childhood, bad decisions in adolescence, drugs, prison. Now they're out and this is basically the only job where they're still willing to hire you even if you have tattoos all over your face and neck. I actually kind of like one of my co-workers at that job. I'll call him Lenny. (That's not his real name. His real name is Rufus M. Clark.) Lenny tried to subsidize his coke habit by stealing from the company where he worked as a surprisingly high-profile investment consultant. He went from living in a luxurious high-rise condominium "with corner windows overlooking Central Park to the East and Lincoln Center and the Hudson River to the South," as he has told me at least twelve times, to a cell with a metal toilet. He has managed to maintain an ironic sense of humor about the whole thing. He actually smiles and laughs. He's just so happy to be out, he doesn't mind spending all day scrubbing dried blood and vomit from bathroom tiles or pulling up carpet where illegal exotic animals were neglected to death.

So, there you have it. Working 60 hours a week, having what's left of my soul gradually crushed into a fine, dry, bitter, flaky powder, struggling from week to week to buy Ramen noodles and the generic equivalent of name-brand breakfast cereals, barely able to contribute my quarter of the monthly rent money. I have no health insurance. I have no retirement savings. I have massive, incomprehensible student loans. I am surrounded 24 hours a day by people who hate me.

With the possible exception of Shay. As I mentioned a while back, I know Shay from one of my jobs—the first one, to be exact, at the restaurant that shall remain nameless. I don't know if you could say she exactly "likes" me, as that might be a bit of an overstatement, but she seems to cheerfully tolerate me. Well, she used to. Before the Incident. Now she won't even make eye contact anymore.

It all started when we were sitting out in the alley behind the restaurant taking a smoke break.

"What the ever-loving holy FUCK," she wanted to know, "is behind the male obsession with knockers?" (She actually said "knockers.")

"Well, I ..."

"Now listen," she continued, cutting me off, "I get it: everyone likes to look at pretty girls. That includes me, and I'm straight as the brass rail at the Royal Observatory in London."

"The one that marks the Prime Meridian?"

"Yeah, that one. As opposed to the other one, dumbass."

"I don't think it's brass anymore. I think they upgraded to stainless steel or titanium or something."

"Whatever, dick. The point is, we all like to look a pretty girls. No matter how straight we are. And trust me, I am, like, *super* straight."

"Yeah, you mentioned that."

"We all like legs and butts. We all like hair and eyes. We all like a nicely proportioned face. Some find all that attractive in an erotic way, and some—like me, being totally straight—we just find it *nice*. I can look at a pretty girl with the same appreciation I have for a sunset or a waterfall. But what's the goddamn deal with guys and tits?"

"What's not to understand? Tits are great."

"Yeah, but they're just a body part. They're part of a whole package. They're secondary sexual characteristics. They say, 'look, this is a woman,' the same way broad shoulders and a square jaw say, 'look, this is a man.' It's ridiculous to take them out of context."

"Well ... don't you like dicks?"

"Sure, I like dicks, but not by themselves! Who wants a dick by itself? I would never pay to see a picture of a dick. I would never buy a magazine with pictures of dicks. I wouldn't subscribe to a Web site that promised new dicks every day. I would never ask my boyfriend to text me a picture of his dick. If I like a guy, OK, I like his dick. I don't like his dick by itself, as a stand-alone feature. That doesn't even make any sense."

I shrugged. "I don't know. Guys like objects, I guess. They like toys. They like to play with things."

"OK, yeah, that is SO not sexy."

"What can I tell you? We like 'em. Some of us like 'em more than others."

She shook her head. "Yeah, but it goes beyond that. It's like a RELIGION for you fuckers."

"We like to focus our attention."

She rolled her eyes. "Christ! Tell me about it!"

"It's not ALWAYS boobs, you know."

"Oh, I know. Guys LOVE to fixate on certain body parts."

"Don't say 'fixate.' It's not a real word."

"It's obnoxious. You have these self-described butt men, boob men, leg men . . ."

"I know a guy who likes feet," I said.

"Yeah, well, that's the thing. It's all about worshiping a body part. Don't you think that's kind of weird?"

"Sure?"

"How can you respect someone as a human being when you are evaluating some specific organ like it's an artifact on display in a glass case?"

"Excellent question. If I ever get a real girlfriend, I'll give you a full report."

She raised an eyebrow. "You've *never* had a real girlfriend?"

"Well, I mean . . . define 'girlfriend.'"

"Like NEVER never?"

"You're changing the subject."

"Have you *seriously never* had a real girlfriend?"

"I kind of thought I had one once, maybe. I *thought* she was my girlfriend. I'm not sure she was operating on the same frequency with me on that point, but you know, whatever. We're getting way off the subject."

"What was the subject?"

"Boobs."

"Right."

"It's a question of perceived value."

"OK, so now this is an economics thing?"

"Everything is economics."

"All right then, have you ever paid to look at boobs?"

I hesitated for a second. "Well . . . yeah. Sure. I mean, everybody has."

"*I* haven't."

"Well, you know what I mean."

"Yeah, I know *exactly* what you mean. You mean the word 'everybody' means the same thing as 'every man.'"

"Fine, fine, sorry, forget it, scratch that, what I meant was, every guy I know—every *straight* guy—has paid, at some time, in some way, to look at boobs."

"WHY?"

"I . . . don't know?"

"You don't have to answer on behalf of the entire male half of the human race. You can just answer for yourself. Why? WHY?"

"I don't know. I'm sorry, I don't know. I just like them. A lot."

Shay released an extravagant sigh. "I do NOT understand men. I don't understand women, either. I don't understand anybody. I just don't get it."

"What don't you get?"

"Any of it. It's all so inherently fucked up."

"Don't be mad at me. I didn't do it."

"I'm not mad at you, Schuyler. I'm mad in general."

"I don't see why. You're a girl. You can get sex any time you want."

Shay flinched at the word *girl*. "OK, first of all: not true. Second of all, what the hell? That's such an offensive cliché. And by the way, it's not that simple. Nothing is *ever* that simple."

I shrugged. "I don't see what's so offensive about it."

"It's the false gender binary I object to. If you're a man you're supposed to be like THIS. If you're a woman, you're supposed to be like THAT. It's the whole Mars-Venus bullshit, and I'm just so goddamn *sick* of it. Can't I just be *me*? Can't everybody just be, you know, whatever?"

"It's not just men," I reminded her. "Everybody loves tits."

"It's true," she admitted. "But some of us just love them. You LOVE love them."

"It's not a big deal to you because you can see them and touch them whenever you want. You can literally play with tits any time you want to. I honestly don't understand how girls can ever concentrate on anything."

"Oh, that's stupid. You can play with your dick any time you want, but do you—never mind, forget it." She shook her head and sucked on her cigarette.

Readers, let us consider the female human breast. At close range. With our fingers.

Each breast is composed of a mammary gland (composed of 15-20 lobules, each drained by a lactiferous duct), suspensory ligaments, fat, connective tissue, nerves, veins, arteries, kittens, puppies, unicorns, rainbows, and happiness.

When you press them against each other, you get "cleavage," the most powerful force in the universe—stronger than gravity, stronger than electromagnetism, stronger that the bond that holds the nucleus of an atom together.

For many centuries, the purpose of breasts (being fondled and stared at) has been well understood. Also, something involving babies.

Girls discover, upon reaching adolescence and acquiring boobs, that they have the magical power to turn everyone around them into douchebags, assholes, and jerkwads. Thus begins the phase of their life (lasting until death) where they are relentlessly bombarded with signals making them feel self-conscious because they lack the right size, shape, color, proportion, density, symmetry etc.—or just make them feel like they are being punished for having them at all.

So why *are* we so fascinated with breasts? Why do we eroticize them? Why do we turn into gibbering jackasses who can't make eye contact? What's the big fucking deal? I dunno.

They are, essentially, inert lumps (for most of a typical woman's life) with a definite and obvious primary biological function that has nothing to do with sex. I've been told that for some women they are very sensitive (in a good way), but for many others they are no more erogenous than, say, the back of the neck or the inside of the elbow. If you were going to devote particular attention to a body part, I would bet that a majority of women would rather you spent your time attentively and devotedly licking pussy rather than playing with boobs like an infant amusing himself with a pair of stuffed toys. That's just a theory. I have very little practical experience in this area.

Long, long ago, in my on-again, off-again college days, I had a female roommate who seemed to derive great sadistic pleasure from parading around the apartment topless. I always tried to be cool, but it was impossible not to try to sneak a peek. Whenever she caught me gawking, she would chide me for being so "silly."

"They're just fat deposits on my chest," she would say. "They're no more exciting than your own stomach fat. Why don't you go stare at that?"

It's hard to describe how it feels when a woman does this. It's sort of like when a person who has something you really, really want—money, let's say—waves around a huge bundle of cash in front of your eyes, cruelly taunting, "what, THIS? You want THIS? Why? What's the big deal?" You, meanwhile, just sit there, broke, wallowing in your abject destitution, both of you knowing that as much as you want to reach out and grab a big double handful of dollar bills . . . you won't. They're counting on it.

Women with nice-looking breasts don't hesitate to show them off in low-cut tops and padded push-up bras. Some even enhance them surgically for thousands of dollars, which really illustrates the importance and significance our culture imposes on something my former roommate dismissed as "silly." I always have to remind myself: they aren't doing it for *me*. Those displays are intended for a) their girlfriends (It's like men showing off their biceps to other men), b) their husbands or boyfriends, OR, if they're single, c) rich, handsome, charming, funny guys. In any case, definitely *not* me.

Who knows? Maybe I wouldn't be quite so hypnotically enraptured by breasts if I had an actual, physical girlfriend in real life. But somehow, I doubt that.

So to answer Shay's original question, I have no idea. No idea! Like so many things in life, it's a complex mystery of psychology, sociology, and biology. One that I will ponder at length the next time I go to the titty bar. But back to my story.

"How much money do you think you've spent, over the course of your life, to look at boobs?" She looked at me accusingly.

I nodded towards her cigarette. "How much money do you think you've spent sucking on the smoke from flaming dried leaves?"

"Fuck you. How much? Give me a number. Estimate."

"I have no goddamn idea. Probably a lot. What do you want me to say? Do you want me to be ashamed? I'm sorry. I love tits, OK? I love them. There, I said it. I love them. I love tits. And women won't show them to me for free, so I pay for it. Alright? There you have it. I've said it. I've probably spent more money on looking at tits than anything else, except maybe my college education, and look where that fucking got me." I looked at the name of the restaurant, which was lettered on the back alley door, with the words, "deliveries only."

Shay shook her head. "Tell me about it. I have a degree in fucking cultural anthropology."

"No shit?"

"No shit."

"Well, ain't that just a kick in the pants. And here we are."

She looked around the alley, at the piles of garbage. The narrow, squallid gap between buildings concentrated the smell of rancid grease and the buzzing of flies. "Yeah, here we are."

I glanced at the time on my phone. The screen was cracked, but I could still read the numbers, so it was slightly superior to my bed-side clock radio. "For another two hours, anyway."

"What are you going to do after work? Go out drinking?"

"Nah, can't afford it. I'm just going to go home and jerk off."

"Got a hard drive full of tits, I'm guessing."

"Tits, yeah. Lots of things, but definitely some tits in there."

"Yeah? What else?"

"Lots of shit."

"Like what?"

I shrugged. "Weird-ass perverted shit. Whatever gets me off."

"So if I went to your apartment and turned on your computer right now and just started browsing directories and opening folders, what would I find?"

I laughed. "I do *not* recommend doing that."

"Question stands. What would I find?"

"I told you. All kinds of strange, fucked-up shit."

"You're evading the question, dude."

"Well, come to my apartment and find out for yourself if you're so curious, Miss Degree in Cultural Anthropology."

"Maybe I will." She paused, examined my facial expression, and then busted out laughing so hard I thought she was going to hurt herself. She took one last drag on her cigarette, then threw it on the pavement and crushed it out. "Oh my fucking god, you should see the look on your face. You know what? My shift ends at seven."

So I smuggled her in. That's the best way to put it. I sneaked her in passed Idiot Roommate, who (thank god) was the only one home at the time, and into my room. I felt bad that I hadn't had a chance to clean up beforehand, but whatever, I wasn't going to let this chance slip by. I was seriously hoping I could at least get a look at her half-naked. Maybe more, who knows?

"Your place is filthy," she said, her hands on her hips, looking around in undisguised disgust.

"Yes, it is," I agreed. "It's not a good place. From a cultural anthropology standpoint, though, I'd guess it was a gold mine."

"More like a shit mine."

"Why would anyone mine shit? By definition, it's pretty much the least valuable substance in the world. People literally pay to get rid of it."

"Not bat shit," she said. "Not cow shit. Guano and manure are highly prized commodities."

"Remind me not to talk to you anymore."

"I'll do that, right after you show me what's on your hard drive."

"I don't think I'm going to just let you explore freely. I think I should at least act as a sort of tour guide."

"Fair enough. Go ahead, curate. Let's start with a breakdown of what there is to see. Give me the full catalogue."

I sat down in front of the keyboard and looked at her. "Uh, how do you want me to list it? Alphabetically? By level of extremity? It's all subjective. I'm not sure how to arrange my fetishes."

"How many do you have?"

"Plenty."

"Well, start with the one you think is the strangest."

"The one I think is the strangest, or the one I think other people would think is the strangest? Or the one I think *you* would think is the strangest?"

"Quit stalling and tell me something weird and fucked-up that I would find on your hard drive, or I'm going to push you out of the way, sit down in that chair and start guessing passwords."

"OK, OK, I guess the weirdest thing is probably all the girls in arm casts."

"What."

"All the girls in arm casts."

"Yeah, I heard you the first time."

"So why did you say 'what'?"

"I was hoping for an explanation."

"Yeah, well, it's kind of hard to explain."

"Try."

"Well . . . I had this friend. Annabelle. I was 13; she was 16. She liked me because I was, um, I suppose you could say I was . . . harmless. Unthreatening?"

"I can see that."

"Thanks."

"It's not a bad thing."

"Whatever."

"How did you know each other?"

"We met at camp. I was a camper. She was a counselor."

"Hoo boy, this is bad-porn material already."

"Hey, you asked."

"I know. Sorry."

"Do you want to hear this or not?"

"I do, I do, keep going. Please."

"Anyway, she broke her arm. I don't remember how. I think she fell or something. Doesn't matter. But she had this cast, and she let everybody sign it."

"Including you?"

"Including me. I remember getting really close to her chest so I could use a felt-tip marker to write my name on the plaster. I was so close. I think that was the closest to a girl's chest I've ever been. I'm *sure* it was."

"So that's where the erotic association comes from?"

"No. Well, I mean yes, that was part of it, but it wasn't the main thing. You see, the situation was, she couldn't get it wet."

Shay blinked. "I don't understand."

"She couldn't get it wet, so the only way she could take a shower was to wrap it up in plastic cling film and then wash herself with her other hand. It was very awkward. She trusted me, she thought I was safe, so one day she asked me to help her."

"Oh my god. Now I totally get it."

"So I did. I went into the shower with her."

"Where?"

"In the bathhouse. Late at night."

"Jesus! Where were the adults? Weren't there, you know, like, supervisors and shit?"

"All down at the lake smoking weed."

"Of course."

"So it was just the two of us in there, in that moldy old campground bathhouse with the avocado-green octagonal porcelain tiles, after midnight, with flies and moths and mosquitoes swarming around these bare fluorescent tubes up above us. It smelled like . . . well, it smelled. Gives me a hard-on just thinking about it."

"Were you naked?"

"She was wearing a white bra and white panties. I was wearing my underwear."

Shay smiled for the first time. "Did her underwear get all wet and translucent in the shower?"

I sighed. "Yes."

"And did you get a giant 13-year-old boner?"

I groaned. "Yes."

"Did she pretend not to notice?"

". . . Yes."

"Could you see everything?"

I closed my eyes and shook my head. "Oh my god. Oh my god. Yes. Yes. You could see everything. It was like she wasn't wearing anything at all. No, it was better than that. It was like she was wearing something that was designed to show off the way you could totally see everything. It was, it was, it was, I don't even know. I can't even describe it. It was so intense."

"So what happened?"

"What do you mean what happened? Nothing happened."

"Nothing?"

"Nothing. I helped her shower. I got her all soaped up, and I helped to rinse her off."

"Did you touch her inappropriately?"

"No."

"Do you wish you had?"

"No. But I think about it all the time."

"How long ago was that?"

"I don't know . . . a long time. Ten years? No, more like fifteen years. Fuck." I did the math. "Jesus, more like twenty-two, twenty-three years. Twenty-eight! Fuck! Fuck. Oh my God. Yeah, I think about it a lot. I do."

"And this didn't seem like a totally fucked-up thing to you at the time?"

"No! No. Not at all. That's the thing, you know? That's the thing about camp. It's so weird, but you get used to it so fast. After a couple of days, it's like you've lived there your whole life. Of course the mess hall is over there, that's just where the mess hall is. Of course I live in cabin 22, that's where I live, it's like I've always lived in cabin 22. Of course that's my bunk over on the left, and of course I'm on top. Everything is just normal, everything is just your life. And of course here I am with this, this, this, girl . . . and she's, and we're . . ."

"So now you look at pictures of girls with their arms in casts. On the Internet."

I put my hand on my face. "Yes."

"OK, so what else?"

"I told you, all kinds of shit."

"Like what? Give me another example."

I sighed. "Well, I have this thing about girls stuck to the wall."

"Stuck to the wall?" Shay looked confused. "You mean like it's covered in glue?"

"Yeah, exactly. Or flypaper. They're naked, and for some reason these naked girls are just stuck to the wall, trying to get away, but they can't."

"All right. What else?"

"Well, I'm kind of into girls that have extra breasts."

"Like that chick from *Total Recall* with three tits?"
"Eh, I like them in even numbers. In vertical rows, you know? Four, six, eight."

"You weren't kidding. You really are into some weird, fucked-up shit."

"Hey, I told you."

"So why don't you fantasize about normal stuff, like getting laid like a regular person, with a regular girl, under regular circumstances?"

I shrugged. "I guess it's because I don't really know what it's like."

Shay looked at the computer. "OK, so show me something."

"What do you want to see?"

"What was the most recent thing you got yourself off to?"

I didn't mention my cam girl, Jekyll. "Well, I guess it would be this." I opened the folder marked, "PRN" and then the sub-folder called "INSERTIONS," and the sub-sub-folder called "FRUITS AND VEGETABLES." I opened a high-resolution .jpg of a redhead wearing six-inch Lucite heels and nothing else, stuffing an eggplant into her vagina."

"Wow," Shay said, checking it out.

"You think it's gross?"

"I wouldn't put that there, but hey, she's probably getting paid a lot of money to do it. I hope she's getting paid a lot of money."

"I try not to think about that. I just try to imagine that she's into it. I mean, I know it doesn't make any kind of logical sense, but . . ."

"And you look at pictures like this and jerk off?"

"Yes."

"Show me."

I accidentally pushed the mouse off the pad and onto the floor. I looked at Shay. "What?"

"Show me. Show me how you do it. Show me how you jerk off."

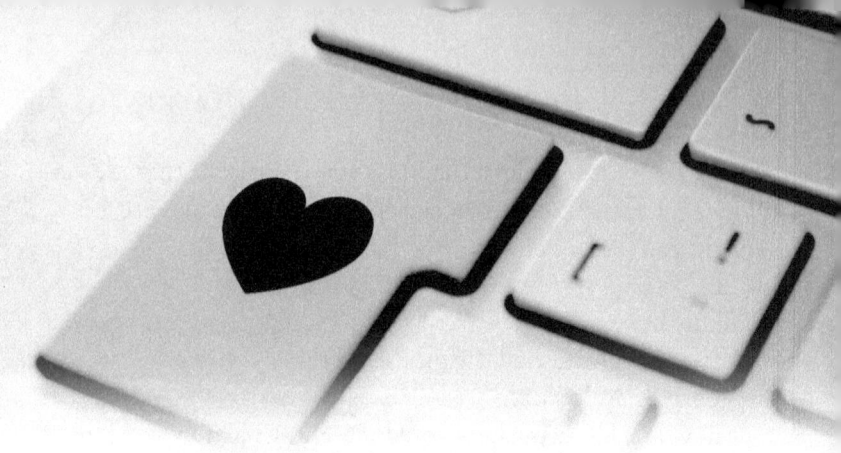

CHAPTER FIVE

Becoming An Angel

CHRISSY

I called in sick that Tuesday. It gave me time to shop for a new dress, since I only had the two black ones and Kevin had already seen one. I needed to find another option.

I shopped at some of the thrift stores in certain areas of the city. The elite of NY considered last season's fashions to be nothing short of worthless when the next season's fashions hit. Some shops didn't always know the worth of the garments that lined their racks. As long as you were willing to work for it a little, you could find some treasures.

I did find two treasures on this particular "hunt." One was a simple sleeveless brown dress that had a gold choker. It would look amazing with a pair of brown boots I owned. I also found a dark green cocktail dress with an empire cut. I decided to wear the green one tonight.

I spent hours getting ready. I shaved everything. I wasn't sure what Kevin would like, but it seemed like being completely clean was always appreciated.

I even matched both my nails and toes to the necklace I had chosen.

Raquel had texted in the afternoon to check on me and see if I was coming into work the next day. I told her I was fine, seemed like I was recovering, and that I would be in bright and early Wednesday morning. It wasn't for any other reason except that even though I got sick-pay, I would still need at least ten hours of overtime to keep me head above water in the rent department.

Since I didn't know if we would be eating, I had a small snack right before eight and made my way downstairs to wait for him. I texted Jess to let her know I was heading out and I would text her details as I got them.

As I descended the stairs, I began to get a nervous knot in my stomach. What if this was totally crazy? What if he wasn't going to show up? I felt myself begin to get anxious.

I knew it was possible to have a panic attack. I had them before, mainly about money and being terrified to live on my own. I knew the signs, and if I opened the door and didn't find the town car waiting for me, I might completely lose it.

As I reached the door that led outside, I took a deep steadying breath, put my hand on the handle, and pushed the door open.

Leaning against the town car was Kevin. He was holding a pink rose.

He stood and walked towards me with that amazing smile on his face. Wrapping his arm around my waist, he pulled me to him and kissed me gently. When he finally separated his lips from mine, he pulled back only a few inches and said, "You look amazing!"

I bit down on my lower lip and smiled. "Thanks." He gestured towards to car and a small, very small, part of me wondered if he was a serial killer, like Ted Bundy. I shook the thought out of my head right away. I was not going to let myself ruin this night.

As I got in the car, I debated asking where we were going. Since I didn't want to mess this up at all, I figured if I asked anything at all, it was possible for me to say the wrong thing and mess it up. So I sat there with a million questions running though my brain.

As we drove, Kevin couldn't seem to take his eyes off me. It was intoxicating. I have never had a guy look at me the way he did. He held my hand in his for the entire car ride, letting his fingers trace little lines that sent shivers up my spine.

When the car finally stopped, we were in front of what was formally a hotel but was now luxury apartments. He got out first and then offered me his hand. He wrapped my arm around his and guided me through the doors being held open by two doormen.

We got in the elevator, and it took us up to the twenty-first floor. The little voice in my head was screaming that I could be murdered at any moment and no one would know where I was. Again, I ignored it.

He led me to a door with the numbers 2107 on it. I made a mental note to text Jess that bit of information. He used a security code instead of a key to unlock it, which was super fancy, and opened the door for me to enter.

This place was amazing. It looked like the pages of a catalog. As I walked in, I found myself feeling like I shouldn't touch anything, it was just so perfect.

Kevin walked passed me and into the kitchen where he opened the fridge and pulled out a bottle of champagne. There were two glasses already on the counter-top.

He popped the cork and poured us each a glass. He walked over and handed one to me: "To your beauty." I clinked glasses and couldn't believe this was happening for real.

"You are awfully quiet tonight, Christina. Is something wrong?" he asked and sounded genuinely concerned.

"I am good. Really good. I have just never had a date quite like this before," I said and tried to keep my voice level.

"Well, I have never met a girl quite like you before," he said, putting his glass down and moving his hands to my hips. I looked back and forth between my clutch in one hand, the glass of champagne in the other, and the gorgeous man in front of me, and I couldn't help but think I was going to spill my drink... again.

Sensing my mounting terror, Kevin grabbed both the clutch and the glass and set them down next to his and then returned his hands to my hips, pulling me towards him.

"I have wanted to taste you since the moment we first kissed," he breathed against my ear. I moaned. He brought his lips to mine and passionately kissed me. His tongue slid into my mouth, and he tasted like champagne. I closed my eyes and ran my fingers through his hair, pulling him towards me.

He ran his hands up my back, and I felt his fingers clasp the zipper on the back of my dress. He unzipped me, stepped back, and with each hand, he grabbed the small straps and helped the dress fall to floor at my feet.

For a brief moment, I felt exposed. I was standing there in a bra and panties, luckily they matched, and a pair of heels. His blue eyes drank me in as he slowly scanned every inch of me.

"My god... You are so sexy." He sounded like he was almost growling. It sent shivers down my spine and again, I had goosebumps all over.

He turned away from me. For a moment, I thought I might not look that good to him and I folded my arms over myself to cover what I could.

From over his should he said, "Don't do that. I like to look at you." I dropped my arms to my sides again. Next he took off his jacket and laid it on the counter, then his shoes. He moved a little slower with his button down shirt, undershirt, and pants. It was magnificent to watch his body emerge from beneath those clothes.

He was perfectly built. He didn't have a single flaw on any part of him that he was showing me. As he turned around wearing only a pair of boxers, he took my breath away. I could see by the tent-like quality his boxers were presently in that he was in fact very happy with the way I looked.

He moved up and placed his hands on either side of my head and pulled my mouth to his again. Then, his hands moved down to my waist, and still kissing me, he moved us both backwards. I was assuming towards the bedroom. I closed my eyes and tried to think about the kissing, while still focusing on walking backwards in the heels I still had on, which is not an easy feat when I am not being distracted.

After a minute, he stopped and then pulled back. He was smiling again. "Lay back on the bed for me, Angel," he said.

I began to step out of my heels, but he stopped me and told me to leave them on. I moved my body onto the bed as sensually as I could. I had never been seduced like this so I had no experience. The thought struck me as I was trying to move myself across the sheets that even if you watch a thousand movies, nothing prepares you for something like this other than actually practicing.

I opted for the sexy cat crawl across the bed. I looked back over my shoulder to see if the effect was working or if Kevin was now terrified.

It was working.

When I lay down, he moved himself onto the bed. Kneeling, he lifted my foot up by the heel I was wearing and began to use his mouth to kiss and lick up my entire leg.

I felt the rush of heat fill me. I have never been treated with so much desire. As his lips touched my inner thigh and his teeth nibbled a little bit, I exploded. I dug my fingertips in the sheets of either side of me to hold on as my back arched and my eyes closed.

I wish I could say that I was one of those girls that screamed or moaned out amazingly erotic things when I first had an orgasm. I didn't. I was actually embarrassed for some reason to make any noise at all when I was with someone. However, I have found that it is basically expected. So, now when I come, I moan, out-loud, very loud.

My eruption only spurred on Kevin with more intensity. He continued to kiss all the way up to my panties, which I assumed were coming off now. I assumed wrong. He put his mouth against the fabric and began to lick and suck.

This was a first for me. I was a little confused, and yet terribly aroused in the same moment. Maybe this was his way of being safe with someone he had just met. I had heard from a friend, the first time one of the guys she had dated had gone down on her, he had used Saran Wrap to cover her naughty bits while he ate her out. So, this wasn't as weird as plastic wrap; it was just different.

It didn't take me long to come again. He knew how to use the perfect amount of lips, tongue, and teeth.

When he brought me a third time, I wondered when I would be able to "return the favor" so to speak.

Then he pulled back, got off the bed, and removed his boxers. I saw the entire package and it was... a little smaller than I thought from the pre-disrobing view through the boxers.

I cleared that thought from my mind as it could possibly kill the mood.

He moved back to kneeling between my legs. I began to sit up when he shook his head very slowly. He moved each of my legs so the knees were bent and the heels landed right next to his calves.

Then he began to stroke himself. He maintained eye contact with me the whole time and it got very uncomfortable. I do not have the confidence to do that. I wasn't sure what to do so I closed my eyes and arched my back a little as if to say without words "this is so hot and I am about to come again."

"Look at me!" His voice hit me with such urgency. It was so husky and raw.

I opened my eyes and it happened. He erupted. It seemed he came all over my ... panties?

"God, Angel, you are amazing." He still had the husky voice. He looked down at the mess and said, "Just stay right there. I will get you all cleaned up." He got off the bed and entered a door that I hadn't even noticed in the back of the room.

I fell back on the bed and several thoughts hit me all at once; however, all I could think was how amazing this night was.

I heard water begin to run. After a few moments, Kevin returned with a wash cloth, but when I started to sit up, he did the slow shake of his head again.

I laid back down and let him carefully remove my panties, still keeping my heels on by some miracle.

"I am sorry I ruined your gorgeous panties." He said as he carefully laid them on the bed so they wouldn't make a further mess.

"It is ok. It was worth it." I smiled back.

He used the washcloth and cleaned me off. He was very gentle in all of my folds. I found that even this touch was still stimulating me.

When he finished, he took the washcloth and my panties to the bathroom and I heard the water run again.

When he returned, he put back on his boxers and reached out a hand to me "Hungry?"

I was starving now. My little snack had not done anything. "Yes!" I said hoping I didn't sound too excited. I took his hand and let him guide me back to the living room where our clothes had been discarded. He picked up my dress and handed it to me and then dressed himself. He even helped me with the zipper.

I was going to ask where my panties were, but I assumed he had washed them off and they were drying. Wet panties would be slightly more uncomfortable then no panties so I just followed his lead.

He took me to the dining room and pulled out a chair for me. He had carried our champagne glasses into the room and set them down.

Kevin then returned to the kitchen and after a few moments returned with a platter of sushi and two plates.

"Hope you like sushi," he said with a little smile and wink.

"I do. Thank you," I said looking at the platter in front of me.

I had only had sushi a couple of times. Mainly because my parents didn't believe you should ever eat raw fish and Jessica was allergic.

We ate and I thought to ask him a few questions but he started first. He asked me all about going to school. What was my dream job? How did I get into being a legal secretary? Who were my favorite artists? Did I paint? Time seemed to fly by and I found he was so easy to speak with.

As it neared eleven at night, a little yawn escaped my lips. "I think it is time I get you home for your beauty sleep," he said with a smirk.

I felt my face turn a little red. I hoped I didn't come off like I was bored.

He stood and offered me his hand again. He helped me up and led me back towards the door. He pulled out his phone and sent a quick text.

I started to walk towards the bathroom to retrieve my panties and he grabbed me around the waist and pulled me against him. "Where are you going, Angel?" he whispered into my ear.

How was I supposed to delicately say that I was going to get my wet panties now? I closed my eyes. Think. Think. Screw it. "Sorry, I got distracted. My mind and body were wandering thinking about what we just did." I hoped that sounded as smooth as I needed it to.

"Naughty Angel," he whispered in that husky tone. "How about I pick you up next Tuesday and we can find heaven with each other again?"

"That sounds perfect," I replied and let him guide me panty-less out the door.

The whole car ride he ran his fingertips over my legs and hands. It was amazing how focused he was on me and just me. When we arrived, the driver opened the door for me and as I was about to get out, Kevin pulled me towards him, passionately kissed me and said, "See you Tuesday, Angel."

I got out of the car and watched him drive away.

As I was walking up the stairs, I opened my purse and checked my phone. There were fifteen texts and ten missed calls from Jessica. I called her right away.

"Are you ok?" was her first question and "What the fuck is wrong with you?" was the next. After a three-minute lashing about how I did not in fact keep her informed of my whereabouts, she asked me how it went.

I told her the whole story from beginning to end. She listened and let me finish the whole thing before she asked, "He kept your panties?"

"Yes... Well I don't think he meant to. I am sure I will get them back next Tuesday," I said, almost defending him.

"Ok. Well then I am happy for you, Chris." And that is why she is my best friend. Her unending support.

The next day Raquel seemed a little suspicious as I was not displaying any signs of being ill. I ended up telling her I had uncontrollable diarrhea. That seemed to stop the questions.

Also that day an envelope arrived for me at the front desk. Now, since we are a law firm, an envelope arriving can cause some at least mild curiosity. They want to know first and foremost that I was not being "served." I wasn't.

It was actually a note with a gift card to Victoria's Secret for $200.00. It said, "For my Angel" and it was signed with a K.

I sent a picture and a text at lunch to Jess. "See, he didn't steal them!" I was on cloud nine and apparently that is actually where an *Angel* should be.

Chapter Six

Do You Like My Cock?

Schuyler

Shay was standing behind me, reaching around me to stroke my erection, looking down at it over my shoulder. "Stroking" was not accurate. It was more like, "flogging." I was trying to do it myself, but she kept grabbing for the controls like an over-eager co-pilot.

I winced. "Hey, easy. *Easy*! You're being a little rough there. Slow and gentle is better at first. I have some lube if you —"

"Do you like my cock?" she asked. "Do you like it? Look at it. Look how big and hard it is."

"OK, that's NOT your cock, that's MY cock, and right now you're freaking me out. You're also kind of hurting me."

"*Look* at it," she said, almost snarling, ignoring me and staring at my boner, which she was pounding furiously with her fist.

"Shay, seriously, seriously! Ease up! Ease up a little there, OK?"

"LOOK at it! Look at my big hard cock!"

"Shay, Jesus, cut it out! Stop!"

I pulled away from her. She grabbed for me, and I actually had to push her back. "The fuck?"

"What's wrong?"

"What do you mean, what's *wrong*?" I pulled up my pants in a hurry. "What are you trying to do, break it off?"

Shay looked mortified, then angry. "You don't want it, is that it? You don't want to come tonight? Fine. Go fuck yourself, asshole."

She stomped out of my room. "Enjoy whacking off to porn all alone, loser!" She slammed the door behind her. I heard Idiot Roommate ask, "uh, who are you?" Then I heard the apartment door swing shut with such force it made the walls rattle. Not that it took much to make the walls rattle in this place. Mice fart, and the walls rattle. My *Lord of the Rings* poster fell off the wall.

I sat down on the bed and put my face in my hands. It probably would have felt good to cry, just bust out sobbing like a little kid, but I was too numb with shock and confusion. What the *fuck* just happened? So instead, I reached over to the bedside stand and opened the drawer. I pulled out her picture.

It was the only picture I had of her. The edges were getting warped from me holding it all the time. I should probably get a frame for it.

Although she was a Polish Jew and took great pride in her ethnic heritage, she had an extremely common, normal, ordinary Midwestern American name. If you searched the phone book of any large town, you would find a thousand people with the exact same one.

She was taller, quite a bit taller than I. But then again, most people are. She drove a genuine antique Volkswagen Beetle, the old kind with the chugga-chugga engine in the back. It was a pale blue color, and she had hand-painted yellow and white flowers all over it. She had dyed her long hair a flaming shade of red, and she had trimmed her dense, dark bush into a perfect little triangle. She meticulously shaved and waxed her pussy so that it was always smooth and bare. (This was not, she told me, for aesthetic reasons.) She had heavy, thick eyebrows and a somewhat large, round nose. She always wore these loose, lightweight, flowing cotton skirts with bright colorful tribal designs all over them. She had small breasts with large nipples and never wore a bra. I'm not even sure she owned one, except a sports bra she used for yoga. The only thing I ever saw her wear on her feet was her favorite pair of wood and beaded leather sandals. She wore a jangly ankle bracelet on her right foot. She had a dream catcher tattoo on her left leg. She wore cute little round glasses and a plastic daisy glued to her hair clip. She had about half a dozen piercings in each ear, one in her nose and one in her left eyebrow.

She came swooshing and swirling into my life like a sudden unexpected summer rainstorm. She didn't mind that I look like the result of a cross-breeding experiment involving a hobbit and a baboon. She didn't mind that I can't eat anything without getting it all over my shirt. She thought I was funny. She encouraged me to pursue a writing career.

She always carried a Moleskine with her and was constantly sitting down to make charcoal sketches or scribble thoughts in her journal. She liked to dance with a hula hoop. When she was ready for sex, she was READY FOR SEX. As in RIGHT NOW. TAKE YOUR PANTS OFF, WE ARE DOING THIS. That was hot, but she had the disorienting habit of saying really strange, random things in the middle of the act. Stuff about stars and planets and the aurora borealis and how we are just the universe expressing itself as two people.

I guess we weren't quite on the same page sexually–she was taking a spiritual journey; I was getting laid. She didn't seem to mind. I sure as hell didn't.

She had a job at the art co-op, but I think she made most of her spending money selling pot. She liked to watch foreign films with the captions turned off. For about three and a half months, she made every day of my life amazing.

Then one day she was gone. I haven't seen her or talked to her in six years. She doesn't have a Facebook page. If she has a Tumblr or an Instagram, I haven't found it. It's like she just disappeared. We have mutual acquaintances separated by about three degrees, so I've heard she moved to Portland. I even have her phone number. But I've never used it.

I put her picture back in the bedside stand. I couldn't do this anymore. I needed to find a real woman to stick my boner into or I was going to lose my mind and jump out a window or something.

I turned on the computer. I knew I shouldn't spend the money, but I needed to see Jekyll. She was the only one who ever acted like she was glad to see me, the only one who talked to me like she didn't have to.

The first thing that popped up when I logged into one of my social media accounts was an ad for a free dating site called Seraphim. "No bullshit," it promised, "just sign up and fuck!" It had a red banner with big bold letters that read "Now featuring our exclusive 100% sex guarantee!"

Perfect.

like his Angel on every single date, with amazing food and good sex, if this was the one issue, I could deal.

Jess was not sure where this was really going as a relationship since I only really found out the following things about Kevin:

He was 32.
He worked in "Finance."
He was a dog person.
He didn't like veal.
He worked all the time.
His favorite holiday was Christmas.

At the same time as not knowing much of anything about him, the relationship was simple. We saw each other once a week, and he bought me new underwear constantly. I had learned that I needed to always buy two pairs if I wanted to keep an actual set for myself.

On the third date, he gave me his cell phone number as long as I promised to only text and to not bother him all the time as he was usually busy at work. I promised and in fact I didn't text him for three days after he had given me the number. When I did, I texted a picture of me in my latest purchase for him. "You like?"

He texted back within minutes. "Please send me a new one every day, Angel. You just made my day."

I did as he asked. When I got ready every morning, I sent him a new pic. I would try different angles and different rooms. The only day I didn't send one was Tuesdays. I didn't ever want to spoil the surprise.

On Wednesday, the day after one of the most amazingly erotic showers I have ever had with a man, I received a text from Kevin. "Are you free Saturday?"

I replied with "For you I can be." I was getting better at this seduction stuff. He replied with "I will pick you up at six. Dress casual."

I was so excited I texted Jess immediately. I had never told Raquel about the whole thing or that I was even seeing someone. If she ever asked what I was doing on Tuesday night, I told her I had picked up a business class this semester. She thought this was great since "unless I was very lucky," my degree didn't seem to mean anything.

I told Jess about the Saturday date and she was very happy for me. She didn't think this was the most functional relationship she had ever seen, but she knew that I was happier then she had seen me and this made the whole thing worth it.

I spent the rest of the week in between the state of "Saturday night can't arrive soon enough" and "I have no idea how to truly 'casually' dress for a date."

What actually ended up happening is I spent most of Saturday getting myself ready. This included hair, nails, make-up that needed to look natural but amazing, and picking the perfect cute pair of jeans and top that still made my body look amazing without the need to wear spanx to shrink it all in place.

In the end, I chose a pair of boot cut jeans, cute ankle boots, and a white sweater. At least, I thought it looked cute and casual. I had put my hair up in a messy bun that took a little over an hour to get just the way I wanted it. I had to plan that if he pulled the bun out, my hair would still look amazing. Careful planning to not look like I carefully planned anything.

I was walking out the door of my building as his car pulled up. Well, as he pulled up driving a car. I was taken aback, but it was a slick sports-car. It only had two seats, and he rolled down the window and said, "Well, my Angel, are you ready for me?" Just his voice alone made me tighten in places. When he spoke to me like that, it would send me over the edge. I was standing there, feeling the wetness pool between my legs.

I smiled back at him and said, "I am always ready for you." I told you. I am getting better and better at this whole flirting thing.

I jumped in the car and for the first time I actually watched where we were headed for real. Although Kevin, using his free hand when he wasn't shifting and kept trying to distract me with his little caresses, took us in a completely different direction then we normally headed. I debated if I should ask him where we were going, but I knew he would simply tell me it was a surprise.

I like surprises as much as the next girl, but it having almost everything as a surprise meant that I didn't have any control ever and I absolutely should never consider trying to plan anything other than what panties I could surprise him with. Kevin had favorites. I couldn't get too wild, but I could make them more naughty. I was wearing just such a pair tonight. They were white, with only a small triangle of fabric over my pussy and the rest small straps holding things in place. I also have a bra that matched which basically meant three small triangles of fabric were pretending to be support.

So, trying to play along with his teasing, I watched the roads. We were heading out of the city it seemed. Was I going to the Hamptons? Actually, I had no idea where the Hamptons were. I just heard about them in TV shows and movies. However, as we continued to drive, I noticed we were following signs for the Catskills. This was amazing!

When we pulled up to his "vacation house," it was something out of a magazine. It was huge. He referred to it as his "cottage." It was larger than any house I had ever lived in my life.

As he opened the door and led me in, it took my breath away. He gave me a small tour; however, when we arrived to the back deck that seemed to wrap around the house, I was able to see the nearby lake. The water glinted in the afternoon light, the sun in the sky and then his arms wrapped around my waist... kissing my neck... I turned my lips to meet his, and I was lost in the most passionate moment of my life.

I knew what heaven was.

In moments, I would discover what Hell was like as well.

It was becoming a little chilly on the deck when we finally decided to grab our clothes and head back inside. We went into the kitchen and I threw on my bra, and as I tried to put my panties back on, he took them and kissed my cheek as he whispered to me, "Those are mine." It sent a shiver down my spine. I pulled my jeans back on and as I was looking for my phone in my purse, I heard a noise coming from his jacket pocket.

"Hey babe... Your jacket is vibrating," I said, pointing to the direction of the noise. A confused look crossed his face and then he pulled it out of the jacket after giving me a gentle kiss on the lips.

This moment was almost pure bliss for me. That was for about twenty seconds until Kevin's face changed from smolder to panic.

"Get your stuff," he said, sounding very rushed.

"What?" I said in the typical way people do when whatever was said didn't process at all.

"Get dressed. Grab your stuff. We have to leave," he said. This time his tone of voice was like nothing I had ever heard before. At first, I wanted to say he sounded stressed but that wasn't it at all. He sounded freaked out.

"What is happening?" I asked. I don't think my brain could process the change in reality that was happening.

Kevin began to throw my clothing at me. "Get dressed." This was an order.

I grabbed my clothes, hastily trying to get them on. When I was dressed, I looked around to make sure I had everything, and he grabbed my bag and started heading for the door.

As we left the house and he threw our bags in the car, I heard the sound of the phone again. When he looked at it, it seemed to panic him even more. He didn't hold the door as he normally did and just said, "Get in."

He tore off out of the driveway.

We didn't say anything for a while. He would grab the phone and read whatever was displaying on screen.

After about an hour, when we were at a stoplight to turn onto the highway to take us into the city, he screamed "FUCK!!!" and hit the steering wheel with his hands.

I started to reach over towards him. I wanted to help or comfort or do anything that would somehow make him feel better. As my hand almost reached his, he turned and I could see in his eyes that he didn't want that. In fact the person who I had started this trip with was now gone. Sitting next to me was not the perfect romance novel hero; instead, there was someone who was scared and angry.

We rode in silence back to the city. When we pulled up to my apartment, I turned for the second and last time to see if the man who had made me feel the most incredible and desired I had in my entire life had returned.

When Kevin's gaze met mine, I knew that at least right now he was gone. I reached in the back seat to grab my bag. He pulled me into an awkward side hug and then kissed me on my neck and whispered, "I am sorry, Angel." Just as soon as the hug happened, the coldness returned and he was staring forward.

I got out of the car and headed up to my apartment. It was late on Saturday night. I put my stuff down, changed into pajamas, and crawled into bed hoping that this would be gone like a dream in the morning.

CHAPTER EIGHT

Becoming A Prize

SCHUYLER

I spent a couple of hours putting together my profile. I found a couple of adequately flattering photos of myself, one of me holding my chess club trophy and another of me in suspenders and a silly hat, holding the trumpet that I played in my high school band. I couldn't find anything more recent than about ten years ago. In all the pictures of me taken since then, I look kind of sad and angry.

In opening my free Seraphim account, my thinking was, sure, I'm gross and wretched, but I'm sure there must be lots of other people out there who are grosser and more wretched, and/or girls who have some sort of psychological disorder that causes them to be attracted to gross, wretched guys like me.

I've been living in New York City my entire adult life. I use the term "adult life" in the sense of being alive and being old enough to vote, drive, drink, and have gum disease. Sadly, I do not use it in the sense of "adult entertainment." If anything, what scant entertainment my life contains is decidedly juvenile. Anyway, New York City has a population of eight and a half million people. Assuming that roughly half of them are female, and some percentage of that figure are in my date-able (dateable? datable?) age range, that means there are . . . I don't know, I'm bad at math, but it's a large number. And yet year after year, I'm alone, which seems to prove that I am perhaps the world's most colossal dork. I mean, seriously, how unappealing do you have to be to remain single for the better chunk of a decade? Sure, all right, I'm not a treat to look at. But then again, I see plenty of dudes who are WAY worse-looking than I am walking around with wives and girlfriends. So clearly, I also have a terrible personality.

Thinking tactically, I had decided to open with the truth. So I explain it all in my profile, right up front: I'm kind of a loser, I'm short, I'm ever so slightly on the morbidly obese side, my hair situation is not great, and I have to work multiple soul-draining, heart-crushing, mind-pulverizing jobs just to stay off the street.

I tweaked it and finessed it until I thought it wasn't too shabby. By then it was late and I was tired. I pulled up one of my favorite go-to whack-catalysts, an image of a topless woman with a plaster cast on her arm, drawing a red heart on it with a red Sharpie, her head tilted downward but her eyes looking shyly up at the camera. She was biting her lip. I came in a Kleenex, wadded it up, and tossed it in the nearly overflowing trash can under the folding card table upon which my computer rested. Then I crawled under the covers and fell asleep.

I woke up at six and the first thing I did after taking a leak was check my Seraphim inbox. It contained nearly a hundred messages.

I wasn't at all sure what to do.

After recovering from the initial shock, I realized that I needed to figure out how many, if any, were legitimate. I assumed that a lot of them were spambots. I also assumed that a significant fraction were hookers. That's fine; I'll check their rates and see if any of them are within my budget. I will also assume that, since they answered MY ad, the remaining non-hookers and non-spambots are either a) desperate and have lowered their standards below zero and into the negatives or b) have low self-esteem and want to punish themselves by being in a relationship with someone who is, objectively speaking, awful according to any objectively measurable parameter.

So now I was honestly confused. Do I attempt to engage them in online conversation? I have no idea how to do this. I don't know the difference between being amiable and being revolting. I don't know where to draw the line. I live with three of the worst people I know. My social sensibilities are shot to hell. True, I did once write a popular blog entitled, "How Not to be a Creep," but it was written from an insider's perspective, and when applied to myself, the guidance has always been simple: LEAVE THE AREA.

What am I to make of women—I assume most of them probably really are women—who are potentially interested in me? It makes no *sense*. The nicest thing I can think of to say about myself, aside from my preternatural ability to concoct brilliant pop-culture puns when no one is around, is that I will never send you dick pics. I have a simple reason for this: I have a very small and unattractive penis.

I now find myself in the peculiar and unexpected position of not being sure how to proceed combing through all these responses. How do I filter them? I have no experience with being selective.

I guess I just needed to dip my ladle in the River of Crazy and see what comes up.

I obviously had to perform some kind of sorting and filtering. I cracked my knuckles, rolled my head to loosen up my neck, and got down to it.

An easy way to start was by deleting everything in a foreign language—a surprising number seemed to be in Russian or Chinese—as well as everything written in all caps and everything riddled with the most egregious violations of spelling, grammar, punctuation, and syntax. Then I weeded out all the ones with profile pics that were clearly just stolen porn. (I recognized many of them from my own personal collection.)

Next I culled the most baldly fake ones, the messages that said things like, "hey cutie, you seem like my type. Want to get together later? Copy and paste this URL into the address bar of your browser."

Then it was a matter of combing through the remaining ones—a far more manageable number at this point—and eliminating the most insane ones. If a respondent mentioned having her heart broken more than six times in one paragraph, she was out. A lot of the messages and profiles were full of rage, ranting about how men were a bunch of jerks and why couldn't there be one guy, *just one guy* out there who was a decent human being who wasn't going to betray my trust, ruin my life, trample my self-esteem, and abandon me? (This rhetorical question often concluded with a string of five or more question marks, which I cannot bring myself to reproduce here.) I could see that if I was going to get any pussy at all, I would have to navigate a formidable minefield.

And then there was the issue of profile pictures. I was automatically suspicious of anyone who posted a photo of a cat or a cartoon character instead of her face. Likewise, I was skeptical of an extreme close-up of only her eyes, or any shot taken from a strange angle or with peculiar and extreme lighting. Another other major red flag was a ridiculous degree of Photoshopping—I often noticed that the areas around a girl's belly and bust were twisted, stretched, and deformed as if she were trapped in a bizarre distortion in the space-time continuum. Sure, she appeared to have tits like Anna Nicole Smith and a waist like Keira Knightly, but the dresser directly behind her resembled something out of a Salvador Dalí painting.

When there had clearly been someone awkwardly cropped out of the image, it gave me the heebie-jeebies. I was especially distrustful when there was only one picture. If it's really that hard to find a good picture of yourself, something is amiss.

There was definitely a sliding scale at work here; the attractiveness of a girl's profile pics was directly proportional to the amount of crazy or stupid I was willing to tolerate in her message or biographical info. A lot of the smart, funny, seemingly sane ones were real dogs. And a lot of the gorgeous ones were raving bitch-nuts. I needed to find someone desperate enough to go to bed with a gross loser like me, but she had to be a least a little bit hot, and not the type who was going to follow me around and be all weird.

Photo captions are a point of particular importance to me. It bugs me when a girl posts a photo with no explanation or commentary. The only thing worse than that is when she posts something stupid and basic like, "YOLO LOL ;-P" or a sparkling animated .gif that says, "PRINCESS."

I think I may have an "Adorable-Chicks-Who-Write-Their-Own-Clever-Photo-Captions" fetish. Honestly, it's so fucking charming when a girl has a) the wit and b) the sense of irony to find the humor in the intrinsically ridiculous act of trying to look naturally, unselfconsciously sexy.

EXAMPLE 1 – BAD:

"Do you like looking at my hot body? I like it when you look at my big, gorgeous tits. I bet you'd like to slide your . . ." etc. etc.

EXAMPLE 2 – GOOD:

"I have no idea why I'm standing like this. It's like I've just had something removed from my butt in an outpatient procedure using only a local anesthetic."

EXAMPLE 3 – VERY GOOD

"These are my mammary glands. Showing them to sad little men like you is an act of Karmic charity that could make the difference between Hell and Purgatory for me."

EXAMPLE 4 – VERY, VERY BAD

"omg im soooo horney 4 u babby how u liek my titys????"

Sifting through the unexpected avalanche and seeing how many were savagely furious and/or terrifyingly bonkers, I realized that if I was going to be successful in my hunt, I was going to have to lie more. A *lot* more. I was not attracting the right type.

I skimmed through a randomly selected cross-section of profiles and detected some recurring themes. They were all looking for something serious, something long-term, something "real," someone to love and appreciate them for who they really were, deep down inside. I was going to have to become that guy. I got the impression that they wanted me to think looks and money were negotiable, but that honesty and loyalty were highly prized. I needed to come across as honest and loyal. That was the key. Shared interests also ranked high on the list, as did a sense of humor. Yeah, right. A sense of humor. That's what they all say. They want someone smart and funny. Sure.

"YOU'VE GOT A MESSAGE REQUEST FROM CONJUGALCONJUGATIONS," announced a cheerful pop-up dialog box.

I groaned. OK, yeah, sure, whatever. I clicked "accept" with an air of futility.

ConjugalConjugations
Hello there, Blandolier!

Blandolier03333333
Hello.

ConjugalConjugations
I just found your profile and I was wondering if I could ask you a couple of questions.

Blandolier03333333
Sure. But first, I want to ask YOU a question.

ConjugalConjugations
LOL, OK!

Blandolier03333333
You're in a desert, walking along in the sand when all of a sudden you look down and see a tortoise. It's crawling toward you.

ConjugalConjugations
Really? You're giving me the Voight-Kampff Empathy Test?

Blandolier03333333
OK, you pass.

ConjugalConjugations
Not to question your experimental protocol, but has it occurred to you that any decent AI would be programmed to recognize that question?

Blandolier03333333
Um.

ConjugalConjugations
Do you have any other questions?

Blandolier03333333
Are you a hooker? Not that there is anything wrong with being a hooker, I just want to know right at the beginning.

ConjugalConjugations
Has anyone ever told you that you're really charming?

Blandolier03333333
No.

ConjugalConjugations
Of course not.

Blandolier03333333
Still want to ask me something?

ConjugalConjugations
Sure, since we're both already here.

Blandolier03333333
I'm here, you're there. We're in two different locations. Presumably. I doubt you are inside my apartment.

ConjugalConjugations
I doubt it too. It was more of a figurative statement.

Blandolier03333333
Well, ask away.

ConjugalConjugations

72% MATCH

What motivates you to use a "dating" site like this one?

Blandolier03333333
Why did you put "dating" in quotation marks?

ConjugalConjugations
I think you know why.

Blandolier03333333
I think you know the answer.

ConjugalConjugations
Articulate it for me, please.

Blandolier03333333
Why are YOU using a dating site like this one?

ConjugalConjugations
I asked you first.

Blandolier03333333
If I give you an answer, will you give me an answer?

ConjugalConjugations
It's a deal.

Blandolier03333333
I am looking for true love.

ConjugalConjugations
Really?

Blandolier03333333
You asked and I answered. Your turn.

ConjugalConjugations
I'm doing market research.

Blandolier03333333
Oh.

ConjugalConjugations
Now that I've given you an honest answer, will you give me one?

Blandolier03333333
Sorry, I was caught off guard there.

ConjugalConjugations
Not expecting honesty?

Blandolier03333333
Frankly, no.

ConjugalConjugations
Well, there you have it. I'm a market researcher, and I'm doing market research. And you're the market, so I'm researching you. What more can I say?

Blandolier03333333
That pretty much seems to cover it.

ConjugalConjugations
So will you give me an honest answer?

Blandolier03333333
OK, what the hell. I'm desperate to get laid.

ConjugalConjugations
How desperate?

Blandolier03333333
Whatever the maximum level of desperation is. Total, absolute desperation. All-caps DESPERATION. Imminent system failure desperation.

ConjugalConjugations
And has this site helped you?

Blandolier03333333
Not so far. So who do you work for? Seraphim?

ConjugalConjugations
No, it's an advertising consulting firm.

Blandolier03333333
How do you like market researching?

ConjugalConjugations
It sucks. I'm an unpaid intern. I have an MBA. I owe $72,000 in student loans.

Blandolier03333333
Wow.

ConjugalConjugations

Yeah. It was the best I could find. I hope it turns into something. Maybe at least a contract job or something.

Blandolier03333333
Well, has it at least been good for your dating life?

ConjugalConjugations
LOL, I'm married and I have a kid.

Blandolier03333333
Oh.

ConjugalConjugations
Sorry, not sexy, I know.

Blandolier03333333
Are you even a woman?

ConjugalConjugations
Yes, last time I checked.

Blandolier03333333
Do you want to ask me more market research questions?

ConjugalConjugations
If you don't mind.

Blandolier03333333
Go for it.

ConjugalConjugations

Age?

Blandolier03333333
36.

ConjugalConjugations
Race?

Blandolier03333333
Formula One.

ConjugalConjugations
Ha ha.

Blandolier03333333
Caucasian. Very, VERY Caucasian.

ConjugalConjugations
Number of sexual partners this year?

Blandolier03333333
None.

ConjugalConjugations
In the last five years?

Blandolier03333333
None.

ConjugalConjugations
OMG, seriously?

Blandolier03333333

Why would I lie about something so embarrassing
and pathetic?

ConjugalConjugations
So you're hoping to end your dry spell by using an
online dating site?

Blandolier03333333
I don't know what I'm hoping for. Maybe a miracle.

ConjugalConjugations
Well, good luck with that.

Blandolier03333333
Thanks. Can I ask YOU a question?

ConjugalConjugations
I'm not going to send you naked pictures.

Blandolier03333333
That wasn't what I was going to ask.

ConjugalConjugations
All right, sorry.

Blandolier03333333
How often do you and your husband have sex?

ConjugalConjugations
About once a week.

Blandolier03333333
That's pretty good.

ConjugalConjugations
Yeah, we have a pretty nice sex life, considering we have a little one to take care of.

Blandolier03333333
I would imagine that does present some logistical challenges. Finding a good time and place and all that.

ConjugalConjugations
You have no idea. And the lack of sleep. Sometimes we're both just too tired.

Blandolier03333333
How often do you think he would LIKE to have sex?

ConjugalConjugations
I think he's good with once a week.

Blandolier03333333
Have you asked him?

ConjugalConjugations
Not directly, no.

Blandolier03333333
Let me give you some relationship advice, from a total loser to a happily married woman, from guy who has nothing to lose and nothing to gain to an unpaid intern with an MBA and a child to raise, OK?

ConjugalConjugations

Wow, OK.

Blandolier03333333
Ask him.

ConjugalConjugations
All right.

Blandolier03333333
Wait for a nice quiet moment when it's just the two of you and you're both in a good positive mood about your relationship, and just ask him: in a perfect world, how often do you wish you could fuck me? It's OK, you can tell me. Be totally honest. His answer might surprise you.

ConjugalConjugations
I will.

Blandolier03333333
Have you ever turned him down?

ConjugalConjugations
For sex?

Blandolier03333333
Yes.

ConjugalConjugations
Occasionally.

Blandolier03333333

Let me tell you two things about men. One, sex is like oxygen for us. When we don't get it, it's like we're drowning. It makes us crazy. It makes us do stupid things. And if he loves you, he is probably burning with lust for you all the time, tired or not. And two, every time a woman turns a man down for sex, it's like a dagger through his heart, especially when it's the woman he loves.

ConjugalConjugations
I think I have all the data I need. Thank you for your time.

Blandolier03333333
Wait!

ConjugalConjugations
What?

Blandolier03333333
I'm not saying you need to have sex with him constantly.

ConjugalConjugations
What ARE you saying? Considering you don't know me and you definitely don't know him.

Blandolier03333333
I'm saying that if he looks you in the eye and answers, "three times a week," or "four times a week" or whatever, you should think about things you could be doing to please him, to make him happy, to make him look forward to that one day a week, instead

of him being all frustrated and wondering what's wrong and feeling rejected on the other six days.

ConjugalConjugations
You are very rude.
CONJUGALCONJUGATIONS HAS LEFT THE CONVERSATION

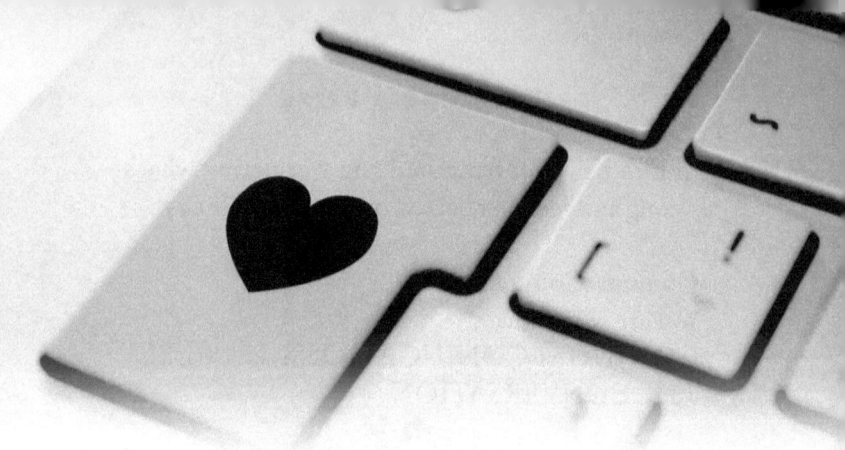

CHAPTER NINE

HEADLINE: I Am An Idiot.

CHRISSY

The next morning, I woke up to find that not only were there not a million roses on my doorstep with an apology note, but I had also somehow managed to lose my phone.

I searched everywhere for it. I grimaced when I realized that I had left it on the counter in the kitchen at Kevin's place when we had rushed out. Worst part was I had hours of driving I could have been playing Candy Crush but instead I was moping over Kevin and didn't think to check my phone.

I needed to call him; there was a problem, however. I had no idea what his phone number was. I began to form a plan. I knew where the apartment was that we often played at.

I decided a shower was probably the best idea at this point. I needed to wash away our day yesterday. I could still smell him and the water from the lake all over me. It made it harder for me to concentrate. I began to scrub feverously to take my mind off what was happening.

As I rinsed the soap from my skin the thoughts that had plagued me all the way back in the car came creeping back in. It was true that he had never actually stated we were exclusive. I hadn't asked either. The water was beginning to cool and all I could think was that maybe he was married. What else could it be?

I wondered as I got dressed if going to the apartment was a good idea after all. If he was married, then his wife might be there. Then what would I say? "I'm sorry but I left my phone at your vacation house while I was fucking your husband." This was not going to end well, no matter what happened.

The worst part was that as I ate breakfast, my thoughts turned from Kevin to the fact that I didn't have my phone. I found myself reaching for it several times. I needed to get it back. I could just go get another one, but I didn't have the money for it, or to call it in as "lost." I knew if I called my parents they would not be sympathetic to my plight. They had some time ago felt that I should be adulting fully and I could no longer call them to bail me out of bad choices, not that I could call them anyway without a phone.

This sucked.

I decided to ask some advice from the person who would judge me the least: Jess. I pulled up my laptop and hoped to whatever power was ruining my life at the moment that she would be online. She was.

Me: Jess, I have a problem.
Jess: Ok. Call me quick.
Me: That is the problem.
Jess: Phone broke?
Me: Not exactly. I kinda left it at Kevin's.

Jess: Oh. Why don't you go grab it from him?

Me: He might be married?

Jess: WHAT?

Me: or not.

Jess: WTF Chrissy? Married?

Me: I don't know. It was a weird night and it will take too long to explain so my question was, can you help me get a new phone?

Jess: He is maybe married?

Me: Possibly.

Jess: And he has your phone?

Me: No. It is at the lake house.

Jess: Wait... What?

I was regretting this now. When you are in the middle of a slight or large panic, reaching out to a friend can seem like a great idea. In this case, I knew it wasn't. Sigh.

Me: We were at his lake house yesterday and I left it on accident.

Jess: Did his wife bust in on you?

Me: No.

Jess: Why do you think he is married?

Me: I don't know. He got a call, flipped the fuck out, and we bolted from the

lake house.

Jess: He said he was married?

Me: No.

This wasn't getting anywhere. There are truly things you cannot do over chat unless you are ready to type a novel. Which I wasn't. This is mainly now because in typing the little bit to Jess I was sounding like a paranoid girlfriend. The kind you judge when you see how they react to the dumbest things.

Me: You know what? I am going over there. I will just ask for the phone back.

Jess: What if you do run into his wife?

Me: That would be awkward.

Jess: Let me know how it works out.

Me: I will

Well, I was correct that she wasn't judging me. Not openly at least. However, I am back to where I was before I pulled out the laptop. I went and got dressed for my little expedition to Kevin's "bachelor pad." At least, that is what I was hoping.

It took me about an hour to finally get downstairs and to a cab. I couldn't decide how to present myself. I decided to go with jeans and a cute top. Hair up and simple make-up. My stomach was in knots when I gave the cross-streets to the cabbie. I didn't know the exact address of the building but this would get me within a block.

The ride seemed to take longer than any of the other times I had ridden there. I figured it was my nerves. I tried to play out every possible scenario in my head. This of course made it way worse. I began to imagine that he was actually married to several women. My mind was spinning, I was sweating horribly, and the cabbie told me it would be a little over twenty for the cab ride.

I handed him the cash and got out of the cab. I looked up at the building and almost turned around. I reached for my phone, which I didn't have. I sighed again and started to head for the door.

The doorman smiled at me and let me in. I considered this a very good sign. At least no word was left to bar me from the premise. I headed up towards the elevator and began to calm down a little.

As I headed down the hall, that bit of calm began to fade. As I neared the door to the suite, I noticed it was slightly ajar. I knocked. Which pushed the door open even farther.

"Hello?" I said sounding meeker then I intended.

I could hear that someone was inside making noise. I took a deep breath and knocked a little harder. "Hello? Kevin?"

"Who are you?" a female voice said back and I heard the distinct sound of heels on the marble floors coming towards the door. I wanted to bolt.

"Umm... Is Kevin here?" I asked still unable to see the female coming towards me. This was rapidly remedied however as the door swung open and a very attractive woman who appeared to be in her late fifties was standing at the door.

"Who are you?" she asked again. This time she had caught me in her gaze, which was penetrating, and it didn't appear like she blinked.

"I'm..." I debated giving a fake name "I'm... Christine." If this was Kevin's wife, he was way more into the cougar thing than I knew.

"Well 'Christine,' I assume you are over 18." she said it as if it was a question; however, it appeared she didn't need an answer as her eyes looked up and down the same way the bitchy girls did in high school. She crossed her arms over her chest. I felt like I was in front of a grade school principal in a way nicer suit than my grade school principal could afford.

She cleared her throat.

"I'm 24?" I don't know why that came out as a question.

"Interesting," she narrowed her eyes. I didn't know what to say or if I should say something. I waited.

"What do you want?" This time it was an actual question.

"My phone at the lake house." After I spoke the words, I knew I sounded more like an idiot than I thought was possible. I was sweating even more now.

"That is too bad. You should go," she said, motioning to the door.

"But..." I began.

"Bye bye," and with that she motioned with one hand as if sweeping away an annoying fly.

I walked out in the lobby to find several reporters now out in front of the building. The doorman came in and said, with his back to the door, "Leave that way," nodding his head behind me. With that, he turned and walked out the door again.

I turned and looked. Near the elevators was an 'EXIT' sign. I turned again and there were suddenly flashes going off. This was most likely a bad thing so I turned and walked out the back door.

Chapter Seven

Bursting Bubbles

Chrissy

Kevin and I had seen each other for a little over two months. Every Tuesday night, he would arrive in his car, pick me up, and we would go to his condo somewhere near Central Park. To answer the question Jess had asked me about a dozen times, no, I had no idea the actual address.

Each night was similar, we would have sex or sexual relations, he would always make sure I came at least two times, and then he would jizz, on my panties, every time.

About the third time we were together, I asked him about it. He told me it is what turns him on. I decided that since he treated me

I ended up begging my parents for a phone. I told them it had been stolen on a subway. My father, of course, was mad that I didn't have insurance on the device and also that I was in a city where I "could have been killed" during the robbery. I told him I couldn't afford it; he told me I wasn't trying hard enough.

The day the phone arrived was the same day I found a newspaper on my desk that had a photo of Kevin and a photo of a sixteen-year-old girl. She was also blonde and curvy. At least he had a type.

Kevin had been arrested for having sex with a minor. His full name was Kevin Thaddeus Mills. He was an investment banker at a very prestigious Wall Street firm apparently owned by his father.

They had, with search warrants, found his panty collection. Apparently, he was meticulous in how he kept track of his panties. He had each in a bag with the first name of the girl, whom he called his Angels, and then the date. A true collector.

They listed the first names of the women and asked us to come forward and they listed a number.

Jess texted me that morning: Congrats on being in the paper.

I sighed. This was my life apparently.

I was happy to think that they didn't have any photos of the Angels. This was until two officers showed up at my work to ask me a "couple of questions."

Because of the nature of my employer, I had to explain why they were here. This began "Panty-Gate" in the office.

I ended up with several more offers from some of the male and female employees to visit the "copy room" after that.

Nothing like finding out that your attractiveness goes up when you are listed with thirty other women as conquests to a pedophile.

I am sure my dad is very proud.

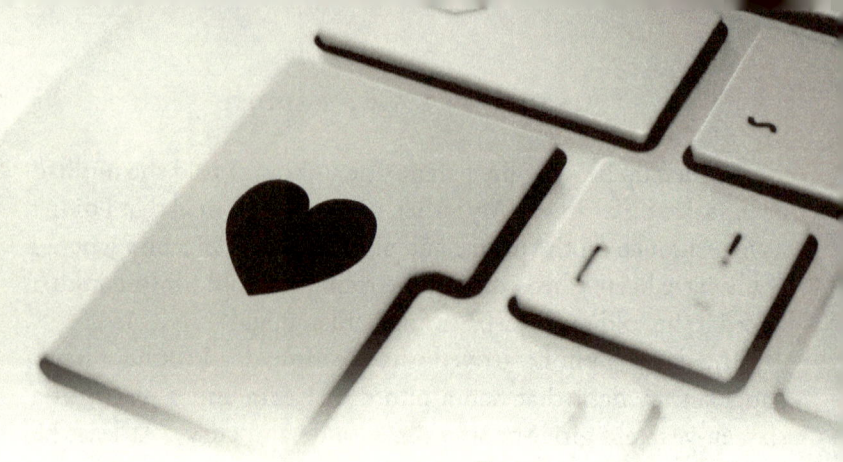

Chapter Ten

Porn Is The Right Choice

Schuyler

My mid-evening browsing session plowed along as unpromisingly as ever. Seraphim was such bullshit. Everything was bullshit. Why was I even bothering with this? Jesus fucking goddamn Christ on a popsicle stick, why don't I just look at some porn and call it a night? But something made me keep clicking. Maybe it was a tiny flicker of hope, or maybe it was just that a neural pathway had been deeply engraved between some primal part of my cerebral cortex and the first finger of my right hand. Click, click, click. No, no, fuck no, no, no no . . . wait. I locked up. My blood turned to ice. There she was. It was *her*!

I looked more closely. Well, OK, so maybe it wasn't her. No, it probably wasn't. It definitely wasn't. Except maybe it was? Could it be her? Who knows? It might be her. But if I can't have her, the next best thing would be to bang somebody who looks just like her. And her status said "ONLINE NOW."

I read through her list of her favorite things. One of them was something called Bierstadt. Whatever Bierstadt was, she said it "totally ROCKS my FACE OFF!!"

On an impulse, I clicked on the icon to edit my profile. "I totally love Bierstadt," I added to my list. What the hell. With a name that unusual, I figured I would give the search algorithms something meaty to chew on. Maybe I'd get lucky.

"YOU'VE GOT A MESSAGE REQUEST FROM ARTICHICK85," screamed a pop-up dialog box, causing my heart to nearly stop. I clicked "ACCEPT" before I even had a chance to think about what I was doing.

ArtiChick85
Hi!

Blandolier03333333
Hello.

ArtiChick85
Sorry, just saw that you were online, thought I'd shoot you a quick msg.

Blandolier03333333
Glad you did.

ArtiChick85
I don't normally randomly msg ppl, I promise.

Blandolier03333333
It's OK if you do. I do lots of things randomly.

ArtiChick85
LOL!

Blandolier03333333
It was my rippling abs, right?

ArtiChick85
Totally. Actually, I saw that you were into Bierstadt and I just had to say something.

Blandolier03333333
Something like "hi," for instance?

ArtiChick85
Something EXACTLY like "hi."

Blandolier03333333
Well, "hi" really does capture the spirit and flavor of what you're trying to convey.

ArtiChick85
Agreed. You really can't go wrong with "hi."

Blandolier03333333
It's a classic. You don't mess with the classics.

ArtiChick85
BTW, I dig the way you enclose your commas within quotation marks.

Blandolier03333333
Is it hot?

ArtiChick85
SO hot. My panties are soaking wet right now.

ArtiChick85
OMG I can't believe I just typed that.

ArtiChick85
That sounded really slutty, didn't it?

ArtiChick85
I'm not a total whore, I promise. LOL

Blandolier03333333
It's OK if you are.

ArtiChick85
Wow, that got offensive quickly.

Blandolier03333333
JK! I was just rolling with the moment.

ArtiChick85
Sometimes I type faster than my brain can filter out the too-much, too-fast, dial-it-back.

Blandolier03333333
I don't mind. I respect a woman who can express herself freely.

ArtiChick85

LOL you'll like me then. That I can def do.

Blandolier03333333
So you're into Bierstadt, huh?

ArtiChick85
OMG, I LOVE Bierstadt!

Blandolier03333333
Before we go any further, can I ask you 1 quick question?

ArtiChick85
UM OK.

Blandolier03333333
You're in a desert walking along in the sand.

ArtiChick85
The Voight-Kampff test? Come on.

Blandolier03333333
I know, I know. Any decent AI would be programmed to recognize that question.

ArtiChick85
Have you had a problem with meeting Replicants on this site?

Blandolier03333333
No, but this place is absolutely infested with spambots.

ArtiChick85
They're probably too cheap to spray for them. How many have you met?

Blandolier03333333
I don't know. That's the problem.

ArtiChick85
You're funny.

Blandolier03333333
I hear that a lot.

ArtiChick85
In a good way?

Blandolier03333333
No, usually more like, "there's something funny about that guy."

ArtiChick85
So what's the longest conversation you've ever had with a spambot?

Blandolier03333333
I spent about eight hours pouring my heart and soul out to a spambot the other night.

ArtiChick85
Was it therapeutic?

Blandolier03333333
Extremely.

ArtiChick85
What did you do when you found out it was a spambot?

Blandolier03333333
By then it was too late. I was emotionally attached. I have another date with her later tonight.

ArtiChick85
You're hilarious.

Blandolier03333333
I'm not going to be all judgy just because someone is artificial. It's not like I'm perfect.

ArtiChick85
So how did you discover Bierstadt?

Blandolier03333333
On the Internet.

ArtiChick85
Really?

Blandolier03333333
There's lots of stuff there. You'd be surprised.

ArtiChick85
So what appeals to you about Bierstadt?

Blandolier03333333
What appeals to YOU about Bierstadt?

ArtiChick85
LOL I asked you first.

Blandolier03333333
Well

Blandolier03333333
You know

Blandolier03333333
Lots of things I guess.

ArtiChick85
It's like you're stalling. Are you Googling Bierstadt?

Blandolier03333333
Ha ha ha of course not. What I like most about Bierstadt is the raw, dynamic, visceral energy of their performances.

ArtiChick85
um what??

ArtiChick85
Are you making another joke? I can't tell.

ArtiChick85
Are you talking about the punk band called Bierstadt?

ArtiChick85
You aren't serious, are you?

Blandolier03333333
Do you think I'm serious?

ArtiChick85
Why do you keep answering questions with questions?

Blandolier03333333
How should I answer?

ArtiChick85
Cut that out and answer me seriously.

Blandolier03333333
OK. What's the question?

ArtiChick85
Are you talking about Bierstadt the punk band, or Bierstadt the artist?

ArtiChick85
Hello?

ArtiChick85
Still there?

Blandolier03333333
Sorry, someone was at the door. No, I am talking about talking about Albert Bierstadt, the American painter best known for his lavish, sweeping landscapes of the American West.

ArtiChick85

OK, that was cribbed from Wikipedia.

Blandolier03333333
No, I'm serious. I love Bierstadt. I love his use of light. I love the idealized romanticism of his work.

ArtiChick85
Really?

Blandolier03333333
Oh, yes. I've always been drawn to the Hudson River School.

ArtiChick85
Me too!!!

Blandolier03333333
They capture so well the boundless youthful exuberance of America in the innocence and optimism that preceded the first World War.

ArtiChick85
Yes, and it's embodied so beautifully in these lush, glowing, majestic natural scenes. Absolutely wonderful. I can't get enough of it.

Blandolier03333333
Neither can I.

ArtiChick85
What's your favorite piece?

Blandolier03333333

Oh wow, it's hard to pick. There are so many.

ArtiChick85
Well, if you had to pick just one to hang on your wall, what would it be?

Blandolier03333333
I'm going to have to say Lander's Peak.

ArtiChick85
OMG I just saw that one at the Met!

Blandolier03333333
What were you doing at the Met?

ArtiChick85
Looking at art, duh.

Blandolier03333333
No, I mean were you there as part of some kind of project or assignment or special occasion?

ArtiChick85
No, I just go to look at the art. Don't you do that?

Blandolier03333333
Of course I do. I do that all the time.

Blandolier03333333
It's just so rare to meet someone else who is as enthusiastic about art as I am.

Blandolier03333333

Most people don't just go to look at the art the way I like to.

Blandolier03333333
It's really refreshing to meet someone who does.

ArtiChick85
When was the last time you went to the Met?

Blandolier03333333
I go all the time?

ArtiChick85
Really? All the time? Me too!

Blandolier03333333
Oh yeah. All the time. In fact, I'm going to be there tomorrow.

ArtiChick85
I'll be wearing a bright red beret. Maybe I'll see you there? ;)

Blandolier03333333
Maybe you will.

ArtiChick85
BTW my real name's Chrissy.

Blandolier03333333
I'm Schuyler.

CHAPTER ELEVEN

A Different Kind Of Angel

CHRISSY

"Another!" I say only slightly slurring my words. The waiter looks skeptical. I don't blame him. Then again there is the small part of me that is wondering if he recognizes me.

Raquel is shaking her head. "We will just take the check." The waiter nods and walks away. I am not sure at this point what bothers me more; the waiter listening to Raquel, who only had one beverage, or the fact that Raquel was again schooling me on everything I had done wrong.

It had been four months since the "Panty-Gate" incident. Kevin was still awaiting trial. I had not been fired but this was mostly because any press was good press as far as the senior partners were concerned.

My parents had found out about the incident and needless to say: dad was not proud of me.

The waiter returned with the check. I attempted to stand up and would have fallen if the waiter, who was a lot stronger than his scrawny frame made him appear to be, had not caught me.

Raquel made that noise she did when she disapproved of me or anyone and we, the waiter included, headed towards a cab.

The rest of the night was pretty much a blur. I woke up still dressed, on my couch, with a note from my roommate next to some Tylenol and a Gatorade "Just in Case. ". With the throbbing in my head, I needed it.

I managed to get into the shower and was just stepping out— the hot water had run out—when my phone began to ring.

I answered thinking it was most likely Raquel telling me what a hot mess I was last night. So, I didn't look at the caller ID.

"I don't need a lecture this morning on the number of martinis one should consume," I said, my voice still a little scratchy.

"Um... Ms. Adams?" The voice was male.

"Who is this?" I was tempted to just hang up.

"Ms. Adams, this is Mike Connells from InterCity Magazine. I was wondering if you had a moment." His tone was pleasant. I discovered most of the reporters who had tried to speak with me since the incident were. However, the way they reported the story was for as much scandal as possible.

"I'm not interested," I said.

"Ms. Adams, Chrissy, may I call you that?" He didn't wait for my reply. "I am not trying to sensationalize this story. I would like to honestly know your side. Tell your story of what happened."

I should just hang up.

Jessica had told me not to talk to any press. She said that no matter what they told me it was just going to end badly. At first, although I was embarrassed about the whole thing, it was kind of cool to be in the spotlight. A couple of the girls had been asked to be on TV shows in the area. I, unfortunately, had spoken only with a reporter at the New York Times. She had started by asking questions about me and how this was affecting me. We ended up spending about three hours together. She bought the food and drinks and I felt it went really well.

Of course, it hadn't.

When I read the article, it turned out to be all about how I could fall for the lies Kevin told and the secrets he kept. It was about how demeaning to women all of this was and if we were not willing to stand up for ourselves, the Kevins of the world would always have the upper hand.

The quote they used, I think, sums it up: "I was happy to know that he wanted me. It made me feel worthwhile." I am not sure exactly when I said this, but I also don't remember how many drinks I had by then.

"Chrissy? Ms. Adams?" His voice pulled me back to the present.

"I don't think so." My head began to throb a little more.

"Please. Chrissy. You can look up my other work. I truly want to tell more than the flashy side of this story. It involves real people, like yourself, whose lives are now forever changed because of it." I wasn't sure if he was sincere, or I was still drunk, but I heard sympathy from him. It was very rare in this entire situation.

"Fine. I am willing to speak with you as long as you promise you will not make me look bad." I figured if ground rules were laid, they would be followed.

I ended up agreeing to meet him later that week after work. I told Jess about the interview. She told me to cancel. I, of course, agreed I would. She can be very insistent when she feels I am making really bad choices. I thought about asking Raquel but decided going against one friend's advice was way easier than both.

I met Mike at a coffee shop. I wasn't about to make the same mistake with the drinking that I had the last time.

We talked for about two hours. He asked me to tell him my story. How had I met Kevin, how had the relationship progressed. He asked a couple of gentle questions about any information I had on the "other women." I explained how I knew there were things that didn't add up, but no relationship was perfect and that I was actually very happy to be part of this one. That is until the end.

I explained the last night Kevin and I were together to him. About losing my phone, the encounter with the woman in the apartment the next day, and the fall-out of all of it. He asked if he could take a couple of pictures of me to possibly use in the story. I let him. I had made sure to look nice but not too made up for the interview. I wanted to give the right impression.

When all was said and done, I felt very good about the interview. I decided I would tell Jess in couple of weeks when she visited me in the city. That would be around the time the article was released and she would be able to see for herself that I could make good decisions.

The time flew by. I worked a lot of extra hours, mainly to have some funds to take Jess and show her the city. It was the Wednesday morning before her visit when I passed by the newsstand to see the picture of me on the cover of InterCity Magazine. I almost dropped my coffee and bagel.

There on the cover was Kevin. It was a picture that had been used several times of him in court, in a prison jumper, hands and feet cuffed. It was taken the day he was told he wouldn't be granted bail. Inset was one of the pictures Mike must have taken at the coffee shop. It was a good photo. The headline however read: Loving a Pedophile. I was mortified.

I bought a copy. I didn't have enough to clear them all off the shelf of this newsstand, let alone the entire city full of them.

I raced the rest of the way to my desk, clocked in, put my headphones, and began to read.

IT WAS MORTIFYING!

Mike had portrayed me somewhere between a Stepford Wife and a porn star. With every word, I became more nauseated. This was horrible. I decided to look around to see if anyone was looking my way. I wasn't sure how many had read the article. How bad was it really?

My phone started to vibrate. It was Jess. I was sure she was going to start her beratement for not listening to her. That didn't happen.

Are you ok? Was the first text.

Need to talk? Was the next.

Let me know you're ok. Was the third.

I grabbed my phone and headed to the bathroom.

You were not supposed to have your phone on you during working hours, but you could listen to music. Which everyone did on their phones now. I don't think most Human Resources were clear on how to handle this, so they insisted your device be in airplane mode. However, unless they caught you, they had no way to police it, unless you were stupid about using it when they were walking through.

I got into the stall. I, actually, did have to pee. In all the movies where they show people just going into the bathroom and sitting, hiding or even eating, I didn't know how they did that without having to pee.

I ended up texting Jess back: *I am ok. I am at work. I will call tonight.*

She replied before I finished the last text: *I am sorry C. I love you.*

I sent back a heart emoji and flushed the toilet.

I left the stall to wash my hands. Two women were there and as we made eye contact, they then looked at each other and made poor attempts to hide their giggling and walked out.

That, it turned out, was one of the subtler reactions I received over the next three days. I was also getting constant calls and text messages from reporters and people who either wanted to meet me or share with me their view of everything they felt on the topic.

Leaving the house was only for work. I had food delivered and simply had to wait for it to blow over. I was lucky that the apartment was in my cousin's name. It meant no-one was camped out front or knocking on my door. So, when I heard a knock on Saturday morning it scared the crap out of me until I heard, "Chris, it's me."

Jess was finally there. I opened the door and gave her a big hug. She came in and I made coffee. She asked me if I wanted to talk about it.

I didn't really.

Instead I let her open a bottle or two of wine and tell me all about the happenings in her life, with her girlfriend and all the weirdness at the school. It was nice to be in someone else's world for a change.

I woke up in the morning when my phone made a weird noise. Jess and I had apparently fallen asleep on the couch in my living room. For a moment I became nostalgic. It reminded me of when we were younger and then I remembered the noise that woke me up.

I looked at the phone and there was a message from someone named: **Blandolier03333333**. There was a little angel symbol next to his name. *What the hell was this?*

I clicked on the message and it launched me into the Seraphim dating app. It even launched open my account **ArtiChick85**. I didn't even remember making the account. I scrolled through my profile and found that it was very slapped together.

"Oh my god," I mumbled. Jess looked over at me. "What?" I showed her the profile. She scrolled through and was laughing. "When did you make this?" she asked, still giggling. "I don't know," I replied but as I scrolled through the messages, it was last night.

This was a whole new level. Making dating profiles when I was drunk. Maybe I was like Dr. Jekyll and Mr. Hyde. Except instead of drinking a potion and becoming super strong, I drank alcohol and became a very flirty art snob. I sighed.

Jess turned the phone to face me. "You have a date tomorrow night."

I grabbed the phone from her and I looked through the messages. I was flirty, funny, and we seemed to have something in common. I looked at his profile picture however and it looked like something from high school.

The other interesting fact was the app had matched us at 72%. This being a new high for me, I knew I had to overlook any reason to pick apart his profile and so I began to read the message.

The message said: I'm Schuyler.

I also had apparently agreed to meet him at the Met wearing a red beret. I closed my eyes, shaking my head. The most tragic part of this conversation with Schuyler was that I had actually purchased a red beret last year and then realized that I was not some super cool French art student and had quickly buried it in my dresser.

"I actually think this will be good for you," Jess said as she stood up to go make some coffee. "You need to move on from the whole Kevin thing and even if he isn't Prince Charming, maybe he will be a good distraction."

I read the texts again. Maybe Jess was right. I needed something. As Jess made coffee, I dug the beret out of the dresser. I could do this, and maybe he didn't know anything about Panty-Gate.

Chapter Twelve

Awkward Doesn't Cover It

Schuyler

I wore my nicest shirt. I put on the best pair of pants I owned. I even shaved. I considered trying to give myself a haircut, but wisely rejected that impulse. Instead, I put on a hat.

Thank goodness it was a cool day because it was going to be a long walk. I didn't even have money for the subway. I schlepped down to the American Museum of Natural History and then took the 79th Street Transverse across Central Park. It was a nice stroll through some lovely scenery on a fine spring day, but no matter how hard I tried, I couldn't bring myself to relax and enjoy it. Few things are more exhausting than trying to convince yourself to calm down. I kept trying to tell myself to just chill and act natural, but that was a ridiculous, contradictory idea. What was natural? Let her see my real self? The truth was not a viable option here. Expose my actual intentions and agenda? That would be a terrible, *terrible* strategy. No, I had to somehow maintain a rickety illusion of decent person-hood just long enough to get my pecker wet and then I could vanish into the safety of anonymous obscurity once again.

I worried, as I approached the Met, that I might not be able to find her. My anxiety proved groundless, however (at least that one tiny fraction of my anxiety), because I spotted her almost imme-diately. As promised, she was wearing a bright red beret. I found myself conducting an instantaneous analysis of her hotness level to establish where I stood, and the results were not good. She was no magazine cover model, but she was adequately attractive, with a rea-sonably nice face and a fairly good-looking body. She was taller than I expected and better dressed. For a moment, I considered bailing out. I could just keep walking and pretend not to recognize her. But it was too late: we made eye contact, and she smiled.

"Schuyler?" (I was impressed that she pronounced it right.)

"Chrissy?" I approached her with a kind of moronic sideways shuffle, like I was afraid she might be a predator. Despite my best attempt to move in with a confident, manly stride, I had the overall bearing of a frightened cocker spaniel with a head injury.

I stuck my hand out automatically, just as she spread her arms to invite me in for a hello hug. I switched from handshake to hug pos-ture at precisely the same moment she switched from hug to hand-shake configuration, and we did this two more times. Looking back, this would have been a perfect opportunity to share a laugh over this silly, funny, awkward moment. But no: we stood there staring at each other in confusion, annoyance, and silence. We never did hug or shake hands. I made some kind of ludicrous gesture as if I were about to pat her on the shoulder or something, but then turned it into a kind of random stretching motion.

She tried to break through the weirdness. "So, hi."

"Hi," I replied, brilliantly.

"How are you?"

"Fine, how are you?"

"Fine, how are . . ."

"I'm good."

"Good. I'm good, too."

"Good. I'm glad you're good."

"Yeah." She adjusted her beret and looked around the way someone looks around when they are trying to get out of a conversation that has been going on for too long. "So, how are . . . um, I mean, are you doing OK? I mean, it's good to see you. Or meet you. It's good to see and meet you at the same time." She paused. "Oh my god," she said, putting her hand over her face. "I'm sorry. I'm not normally this much of a dork."

"I'm not either," I told her, which was a huge lie.

"So, you want to go inside?"

This was exactly what I had been afraid of. The cost of admission to the New York Metropolitan Museum of Art was $25, and I only had a couple of bucks in my pocket. In anticipation of this moment, I had rehearsed my response.

"You know, I've been in there so many times lately, I was thinking maybe we could just go for a walk, maybe get something to eat. You know, walk and talk. And eat. Or walk and eat. Or eat and talk. Or, you know, yeah."

Chrissy looked disappointed. "You don't want to go in?"

"No, no, no. I'd love to go in, but, it's just, the thing is, I think I'd probably be so distracted looking at all the art that's in there, I wouldn't be giving you the attention you deserve. There's a lot of art in there."

"Oh, wow. That's really very sweet."

"Well, you know, I'm really a very sweet guy."

She made a small sideways shrugging gesticulation, the kind of motion a person does when acutely aware of the need to make a clear gesture and unable to decide what kind of gesture to make. "All right then, let's . . . walk, I guess."

I put out my hand as if I were going to offer it to her, but then realized how idiotic and presumptuous that seemed, so I extended my elbow. What was this, senior prom? So I retracted it. Chrissy, meanwhile, had made a small effort to reach for both my hand and my elbow, and now she had her hand out in the air, so I kind of waved at her and she kind of waved back. Then we started walking up 5ᵗʰ Avenue towards the Guggenheim, not looking at each other.

"So what do you do?" she asked after an uncomfortable pause. It felt like a job interview.

"I'm a writer," I said, which was not entirely false, just mostly.

"Really? Wow! That's very cool. So what do you write?"

"Well, I mostly do commercial work right now. But I'm trying to break into the screenwriting business."

"Yeah, you and half of New York," she laughed. Then she looked at the expression on my face and seemed embarrassed. "No, I was just kidding."

"It's fine, it's fine, don't worry about it. And it's true. Everybody in New York has a screenplay. You hail a taxi, you tell him you know somebody who knows somebody, he pulls out a copy from under the seat and hands it to you."

Chrissy giggled.

"Anyway, yeah. Maybe one of these days I'll get lucky."

"So what are your screenplays about? If you don't mind me asking."

"No, not at all. I have this one concept for a movie about a guy who works for a record store. Like real records, you know, like vinyl discs. Anyway, his clientele consists entirely of people who own nothing of value except for these albums. And some of these are, like, rare collectible shit. Right? So the store offers financing for customers who can't afford to pay cash for the records they want. And this guy, his job is, he's the repo man for the records people bought but they're behind on the payments. He breaks into their apartments and steals them back and returns them to the store."

Chrissy busted out laughing hysterically.

"What's so funny?" I asked.

"I'm sorry. I mean, I thought . . . So this is supposed to be a comedy, right?"

"No, this is serious."

"Oh."

"You think it's funny?"

"Well, I thought, I mean, you know, it seemed like it was supposed to be funny."

"Some people can't afford to buy records. So they take out a loan."

"Yeah," she said, "I get that. It's just that . . ."

"They have priorities. They can't afford groceries, but they buy records. It's supposed to be poignant. And this record repo man, he's a tragic figure, profiting from the misfortune of others."

Chrissy, trying not to laugh, snorted.

"What?"

"No, nothing. It's just . . . 'Record repo man.' I'm sorry."

"Well, anyway."

"Yeah, so. It's a good idea. I like it. Really."

"So what do *you* do?"

"Well . . ." She hesitated. "You want to get something to eat?"

"Sure." I pointed towards a nearby cart. "Can I buy you a hot dog?"

"Um, sure. I was thinking of maybe sitting down somewhere, but whatever."

I tried to seem nonchalant. "Well, you know, I kind of like walking with you. It's such a nice day, don't you think? And besides, you're very interesting."

"Yeah, sure. All right."

"So what do you do?" I pressed again as we approached the hot-dog cart.

"I work in a legal office," she said with a sigh.

"Better than working in an illegal office," I pointed out before I could stop myself.

"Right. It's just something I sort of fell into. I have a friend who was doing it. She encouraged me to go back to school to do it. My real degree is in art history."

"Art history," I snorted. "Not a lot of call for that among the Fortune 500 companies, huh?" I gave her a nudge with my elbow. She frowned at me, looked like she was about to say something, then shook her head and turned to hot-dog guy. "One beef dog, please. Mustard and relish. Extra onions."

"You got it," he said and then looked at me. "And for you, buddy?"

I was surreptitiously checking out the money situation, fingering the bills and coins in my pocket. "Hmm, you know what," I mumbled. "I think I'm good."

Chrissy looked at me like I was from outer space. "What, you're not even going to eat with me here?"

"No, no! That's not what I meant. I just, um . . ."

At that moment, she seemed to look right passed me—at something behind me. I guess she was just disconnecting from the situation. Her face seemed to register some kind of shock and horror, as if she had seen a ghost in broad daylight. I guess what she had really seen was ugly reality settling in. What had made me think I could pull this off?

"Well, I'm sorry you find me so excruciating to be around," she said with great suddenness, the way you do when you have to catch a train as it's leaving the station. "Hey, you know what? Just forget it. I gotta go." She spun around and walked away with her hands in the air.

"Wait," I started to say, trying to come up with something to follow up with. But nothing occurred to me. Wait . . . why? Wait . . . for what? So I let her walk away.

"You want your hot dog?" the guy called after her. She didn't answer.

He shrugged at me. "So . . . you want this?" I looked at it, looked at Chrissy walking away, and then looked at the hot dog again. "Yeah," I said. "Sure." I took it with a sigh. There was no way I could get any lower than this, I thought. This was really rock bottom. I turned around, about to take a bite, and spotted Mean Roommate coming down the sidewalk from the other way. I moved to conceal myself, hoping he hadn't spotted me.

"Chrissy?" he said, walking right passed the hot dog cart. "Chrissy, is that you?"

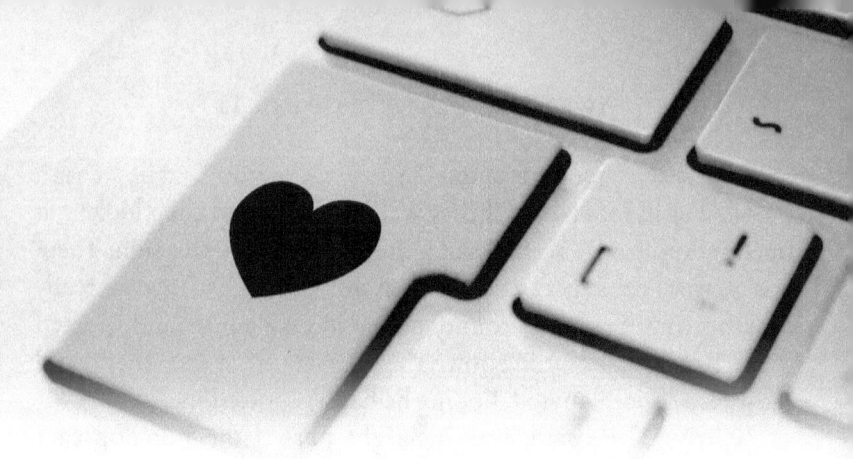

Chapter Thirteen

Karma Must Hate Me

Chrissy

I turned to look back after a moment to see if he was watching me walk away. It's pathetic, but some small part of me wanted him to rush after me. I think that is the whole thing about wanting to be wanted even if what wants you is not something you want.

He was looking down at the hot dog and Sean, this was Sean #1 for those keeping track, was moving behind him. "Chrissy?" he was screaming. "Chrissy, is that you?"

I took off running. I rounded a corner and jumped into the hedge, an actual hedge, and held my breath while waiting for him to pass.

The date was horrible. Schuyler looked nothing like his photo, which must have been taken over ten years ago. He was fat, and not a little overweight, but actually fat. His clothes were terrible, and when he pulled out the couple of dollars to pay for the hot dog, it wasn't even in a wallet but actually just loose change.

Although a distraction would have been nice, this was more of a disaster.

Walking the rest of the way home, my mind wandered to my encounter with Sean #1. I had met him at a bar one night. He was shooting darts with some friends. I had gone with a couple of friends from college.

The bar was one of those bars that everyone from college knew about. Served cheap beer and you could just hang out. I had a few beers, the thought that this might be a pattern with me was pushed aside. I was looking around the bar. At the time I thought was interested; however, I think what I was really doing was looking to see if anyone was looking at me.

I am not sure if the recent events gave me cause for this reflection, but I was getting a worse and worse opinion of myself. I needed appreciation from others to feel like I was worth something.

I knew this more than ever since the moment I laid eyes on Schuyler. I was repulsed, but I was willing to try to find something about him to like so long as he liked me.

This was also true the night I met Sean #1.

He had been playing darts with some other guys. I would say his friends, but I never actually talked about it with him and if he knew them or just met them. This was of course not important.

I was staring at him when he looked my way and gave me the head nod. I call it the head nod because it seems to be a signature move for most guys who are just looking for a hook-up. I really should have looked away at that moment, but the attention was welcome so I smiled and bit my lip.

This was also a signature move. I am not sure exactly what it is about the lip-biting, but it somehow equals sex to guys.

He said something to the guys he was with and handed them the darts and headed over. He was a big guy. I could tell he worked out a lot. He had shorter brown hair, and he was wearing a t-shirt which was very tight against his skin and jeans.

As he approached, I could see that he had a bit of acne and I wondered for a moment if his size was related to steroids. It probably was, but I didn't care.

"Hey gorgeous," he said. "Can I buy you a beer?" I swooned. It was like a drunken spell but the moment he said "Gorgeous," I was done for.

He waved the waitress down and ordered a couple more beers. He asked me if I was in school here. I told him I was. He said he worked at a gym close to here. I think I was a little more drunk than I thought because the conversation became a little blurry and I remember leaving the bar and walking to my dorm room.

In a flurry of clothing removal, he was suddenly on top of me. There was some kissing, which was messy, and then I remember he squeezed my tits and then he slid his finger inside of me. Well, I thought it was his finger. When I looked down between my legs, I discovered that it was not a finger and he was in fact inside of me.

I am not sure the expression I had on my face, but he asked, "Do you like that, baby? Do you wanna watch?"

My first and only thought was 'NO' to both of those questions. Not only was he so small I could barely feel the penetration, he was also sweating profusely as he pounded away at me.

I closed my eyes and knew that I would have to wait for this to be over. I decided to do my best to help it along by letting out a few moans of encouragement. It actually wasn't that long before he made a grunting noise and his slick body landed on top of me. It was gross.

Even worse was after he recovered, he moved so he was spooning me and kissed my ear a little before falling asleep. It was wet, cold, and sticky. A shiver went up my spine as I was walking as it was by far one of the worst experiences of my life.

Not only was it one of the worst but it lasted for hours. At some point, I actually fell asleep. I was surprised he didn't snore, which would have somehow made it even worse. I woke up to him kissing my neck and the feeling of him trying to slide himself inside me again.

"Good morning, Gorgeous? Do you like anal?" he whispered in my ear.

The magic of the word "Gorgeous" had faded with the morning light. Also, his breath that was wafting over me was disgusting. But the weirdest part of those few seconds after he asked me that was the thought that if I was going to try anal sex, which I hadn't to this point, he would be a good candidate as his penis would be the least likely to hurt going in. Alas, the thought of anything penetrating my ass was not appealing.

"Umm... No," I whispered back. "I don't like anal."

"I understand, baby. That's ok," he said as he moved my legs apart. Somehow, my lack of anal willingness seemed to make him think I was ok for a round two. I wasn't.

Before he could get too far into the idea this would continue, I threw the covers off said, "I think I am going to be sick," and headed to the bathroom.

Looking at myself in the mirror was even more horrifying than I thought. The fact that Sean #1 still wanted to stick his dick inside of me wasn't giving him a lot of credit. I needed to get him to leave before I did anything else I regretted.

I sat down to pee and to add insult to injury, there was a condom stuck to my thigh. Seriously, this couldn't actually get worse. I regretted the thought right after it exited my brain. This could get worse and it seemed that every time those words were uttered, it actually did get worse.

I stood up and cleaned myself off as best as I could. I walked out of the bathroom and he was still waiting for me on the bed, stroking himself.

"I'm late for class," I said as I slid on a pair of jeans, a t-shirt, and grabbed my jacket while heading for the door.

"I can make you late for a lot of things." His words actually made bile rise in my throat.

"Umm... no thanks," I said as I walked out the door. I actually hoped I had not given him my number as I made my way down the hall. I waited outside until he left. I had to clean everything including myself and I avoided that bar for the rest of my time at school.

I wish I was one of those people who can say that I regret nothing in my life. However, that I regretted. Along with most of the other men I have slept with. I decided to push the replay of the night and subsequent clean-up from Sean #1 out of my mind and pulled out my phone blocking Schuyler's profile and adding the "X" next to his name in my phone so I wouldn't call him again.

CHAPTER FOURTEEN

The Freebie

SCHUYLER

Thank God the next day I had a cleanup job. I spent ten and a half hours with two other guys pulling bug-infested, shit-stained, germ-riddled garbage out of a third-floor walkup in Queens, including two crusty mattresses and a closet full of filthy, moldy laundry that had become a nest for mice. We pulled up the carpets, ripped apart a rotten dresser, and scooped up the remains of some disintegrating improvised furniture. The original tenants had long ago split, and the most recent inhabitants had probably been a homeless family. We found a coffee can full of the stubs of emergency candles that they had probably been using for cooking, and lots of discarded food cans. They had a bucket they had been using for a toilet. We found lots of cigarette butts and remnants of miscellaneous drug paraphernalia, including syringes that we picked up with tongs and dropped into a box we carried for just such a purpose. Broken glass, splintered boards, chunks of blistered plaster, and rusty nails covered the floors and every horizontal surface. We hauled everything down the narrow stairway and threw it in a construction dumpster the landlord had brought in. The hard work was a welcome distraction, and at the end of the day, Paul the contractor handed me a much-needed envelope full of cash.

I knew I should have used it to buy food and contribute my share of the month's rent, but I needed to remind myself what a woman's body felt like. So I changed clothes, cleaned up as best I could with wet paper towels, and took the bus from the job site to a titty bar called Louie D's. You couldn't actually tell that it was called Louie D's by any of the exterior signage, which consisted of slightly crooked fluorescent green lettering that spelled out:

!LIVE! "Nude"
Alongside those words was a flashing red neon sign that said, "GIRLS GIRLS GIRLS," except that the IRL in the middle one was busted, so it actually said, "GIRLS G   S GIRLS" most of the time, except when the third L blinked on, and then it briefly said, "GIRLS G LS GIRLS."

I pushed the squeaky door open and a blast of cool, stale, cigarette smoke-laden air hit me, along with the familiar, comforting sound of "Cookie" by R. Kelly surging from the jukebox. It was good to be back in a place where things made sense to me.

It was dark inside. I paid the cover charge to a fat, sleepy-looking man on a stool and then went right up to the foot of the stage. A girl with tattoos was grinding on the pole. I didn't recognize her; I guess it had been a few months since I'd been in. She smiled down at me and squeezed her tits.

The cocktail waitress came over immediately. I ordered a shot of tequila and gave her a $20 to break into singles. She came back with a tiny glass that looked like it hadn't been washed, maybe ever, about half-full with the worst-tasting off-brand tequila-ish liquid available, along with a stack of one-dollar bills. I thanked her and gave her two of them for a tip, along with a five for the thimble full of agave-scented turpentine.

It didn't take long for another dancer to approach me. She dropped a small white towel on the chair next to mine and flopped her ass on top of it. Then she offered me her hand. "Hi! I'm Rose. Do you mind if I sit here?"

"Hi, Rose." I shook the tips of her fingers. "I'm Schuyler."

"It's nice to meet you, Tyler. Buy me a drink?" The cocktail waitress was already standing right behind her.

I sighed. "Sure."

Rose whispered something to the cocktail waitress, who nodded. "And anything else for you, honey?"

I slammed the tequila and made a face. "What the hell. I'll take a beer. Anything you have in the bottle."

"We got Bud, Bud Light, Miller Light, Coors, Coors Light . . ."

"Bud's fine," I said, and she left.

"Are you from around here, Tyler?" Rose asked before there could be a lull in this scintillating discourse.

I opened my mouth to reply, but I was cut off by the sound of Mikka's voice. "Damn straight he is!"

I grinned and jumped up out of my chair. "Mikka!"

She gave me a big hug. "Good to see you again, Schuyler. Been a while."

"I didn't know you were back to working here."

"Yeah, since a couple weeks ago."

"How's Terrell?"

"He's doing just great. Just celebrated his fourth birthday."

"Four years old! Wow."

"Yeah, they grow up so fast. It's amazing. You blink and you miss it. Hi, Rose."

"Hi, Mikka."

Mikka leaned in close to my ear so that I could hear her over the sound of "West Coast" by Lana Del Rey. "Were you about to get a dance from Rose? I don't want to —"

"Oh, no, no," I said quickly, just as the cocktail waitress returned with my beer and Rose's mystery beverage. I gave her another twenty and told her to keep it. My money was dwindling fast; I had planned to sit at the stage and milk my stash for at least a half-hour's worth of songs, but clearly that was not going to happen."

"Listen," I said to Mikka, "are you available for a dance?"

"Absolutely," she said. "You ready now?"

"Definitely."

"OK, let's go." She led me to the row of couch-like plastic chairs that lined the back of the club, against a wall of smudgy mirrors.

I grabbed my beer and waved goodbye to Rose. "It was nice to meet you." She frowned and ignored me.

Mikka sat me down in one of the big chairs. I took a drink of my beer. It didn't taste like anything, but it was cold. The cocktail waitress had followed us. She looked at me and pointed at Mikka.

"You want anything?" I asked.

She waved the cocktail waitress away. "I don't need nothing right now. Thanks, though. We can wait until the next song if you want. So how you been?"

"Good. I'm good." I groaned. "OK, that's bullshit. Life totally sucks donkey balls right now."

Mikka laughed. "Yeah, I hear you." The next song started. It was "Don't Cha" by the Pussycat Dolls. "Hey, you ready for a dance?"

I smiled and nodded way too eagerly. I sat back low in the chair and she climbed on top of me, straddling my hips, and reached around behind her back to unhook her bra. Louie D's might not be the cleanest or the classiest joint in the City, but they knew how to break the rules, and that's what I was there for. The usual ordinances pertaining to what you could show and what you could touch were never enforced here. That's why I love cheap, sleazy titty bars. Those fancy places with bouncers in tuxedos and ferns in brass planters, they follow the local laws and don't allow any funny business. In a shithole like Louie D's, though, anything goes.

Mikka lowered herself down on top of me, smashing her beautiful, nice-smelling body into me, pressing her tits against my face. "So what's going on that's so bad?" she wanted to know.

I ran my hands up and down her sides and around to her ass as she gyrated. I told her everything. I told her about Shay, I told her about Seraphim, I told her about Chrissy. I just blurted it all out. It felt good. I couldn't stop. I don't think there is anyone else I could have told. I certainly couldn't have said it to a psychiatrist or a counsellor, sitting in an office under bright lights with framed diplomas hanging on the wall.

"Don't Cha" ended and "Closer" by Nine Inch Nails started. Mikka kept on dancing. I opened my mouth, about to ask her to take a break, because I wanted to stretch my cash just a little bit longer.

"This one's on the house, baby," Mikka said with a wink, continuing to rotate her hips against my crotch. "I've met a lot of guys with sad stories, but let me tell you something. If any dude ever deserved a freebie, it's you."

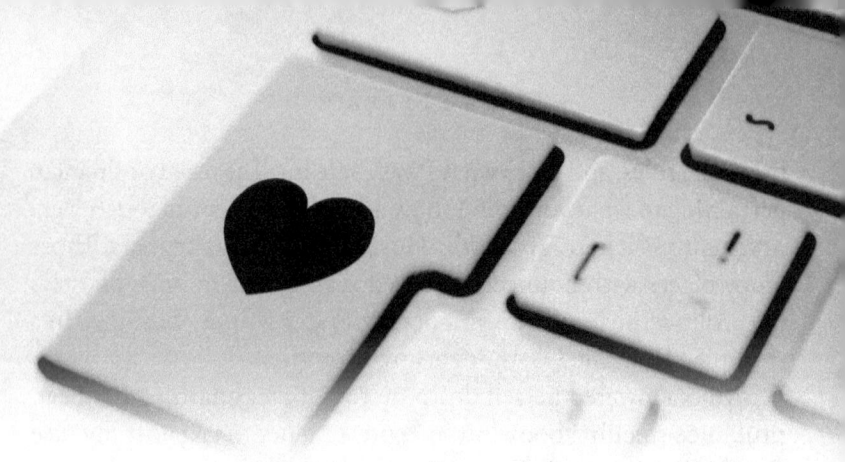

CHAPTER FIFTEEN

The Pity Invite

CHRISSY

I had told Jess what had happened with Schuyler. She thought my judgement of his weight was horrible and offensive.

I tried to explain that it wasn't that he was just fat. She stopped me there are told me that I was being overly critical and that if he wasn't my type to simply say that and to stop calling him a "fatty" since I hated being called that in school.

This was one of those moments where I wondered if the reason I was critical was the criticism I received growing up or if it was also almost running into micro-penis-Sean that pushed me over the edge. Needless to say, I removed the X next to Schuyler's name in my phone. I certainly wasn't intending to go out with him again, but at least I felt like I might have made up a little for the "fatty" comments.

Jess thought that maybe I should take a break from the whole dating thing. I think this was her very nice way of saying that since I was failing so miserably at it, at least the last one hadn't landed me as front-page news, that I should try to let it happen "organically."

When I tried to point out that the last "organic" relationship I let develop was with a pedophile, she simply said that it had a bunch of red-flags and if I paid more attention to them I wouldn't end up in the same situation.

I, of course, did not want to explain that she had encouraged me to ignore all the red-flags with the last one, but that would mean I would have to also admit the red-flags I hadn't told her about and I wasn't ready to fall on that sword.

So, I did just that. I actually went out and bought myself a new vibrator, the kind that has suction for your clit. Since it was almost two-hundred dollars, I felt that I should be able to count on it in times of need.

I was quite sure that in my hiatus from trying to find Mr. Right that it would serve me well and quite frankly, it did. However, it was no substitution for the real thing.

It is not simply about the coming.

As a strong empowered female, you tell yourself that you don't need a man. This is probably true for most actually empowered women. I am not one of those women.

What I want is someone to hold me and kiss me and tell me that I am the most amazing person in the whole world. That I am the sexiest woman they have ever seen and that they simply cannot live without me. I actually wish this was a desire and not the truth which is that I cannot help but identify myself as needing a man to make me feel whole.

Just thinking this, I know that there is a gang of feminists that want to beat me with my new two-hundred-dollar vibrator and choke me with my Victoria Secret push-up bra.

As I was deciding how many bottles of wine I needed to buy to make me forget what a horribly worthless as a female on planet earth, I got a text from one of the girls at work. She told me there was a party for another co-worker. She said it was BYOB but there was going to be music, food, and cake.

Hanging out with my co-workers hadn't always ended well, but drinking alone seemed to be a sign of things far worse.

So, I got dressed in my semi-slutty casual wear, went to the corner store for a generic bottle of vodka, and caught a cab.

When I arrived, the party was already going, music was loud, and so many drinks were flowing. I brought the bottle into the kitchen where a woman in an extremely tight white t-shirt told me to add it to the others and pointed to a counter near the stove that had so many bottles lined up that I was able to slide mine in the back so that my cheapness wasn't evident. The tight t-shirt then pointed to the fancy wine cooler, a beer cooler, and handed me a red solo cup and told me there were a couple different types of punch. I thanked her and walked into the dining room where in fact there were five different kinds of punch to be exact. Each a different color.

"Well hello, Miss Chrissy," a voice said from behind me. It was Mitchell.

I could tell he was a little drunk as he looked me up and down and smiled.

"Don't you look nice tonight," he said as if he wanted to take a bite. He hadn't spoken to me since bending me over the copier.

"Thanks," I said. I sucked at being witty. I looked at the punches trying to decide how to block this out. He moved to stand right behind me "This is familiar," he whispered. "You should try the blue one," and he pointed with the hand holding his cup and grabbed my ass with the other.

I pushed him back and instead of throwing down my cup and marching out of the party with my dignity intact, I walked over to the orange bowl, filled my cup, and drank half of the contents which tasted horrible, filled it again like a drunk college girl, and stormed into the party. I'm such a badass.

I think the "orange punch" was a mixture of several alcohols that didn't combine well that were flavored with too little orange soda so that the overall taste was that of moldy-ass.

Mingling at this party wasn't that easy as it turned out I only knew three people there. The party was hosted by one of the guys in the office I didn't speak to, mainly because he was a pompous ass and had a look of judgement on his face every time he saw me. He also made advances at almost everyone in the office under the age of thirty with the exception of myself.

Then there was Michelle, who had invited me to the party. When I walked up to her to thank her for the invite, she was pleasant, but it took about twenty seconds to see that she had sent the invite not because she wanted me to come. She had sent it so if I heard about the party at work on Monday, I wouldn't feel slighted.

I had ended up with the pity invite. It wasn't, as it turns out, BYOB either. She told me that because she thought it would make it more unappealing for me to come. People who send pity invites have never received one themselves. Worse than not being invited to a party is being invited where you are not wanted.

This made me refill my cup again. I switched to the straight vodka. It wasn't any better.

Mitchell tried to be sly and approach me several more times. One time in the hallway he pushed me up against the wall and began kissing me. For a moment, I found myself kissing him back. This was of course until he said, "I remember how your ass looked bent over in front of me." Even drunk me couldn't do this, again, with him.

I pulled out my phone and knew I had to find someone to come to the party and at least get me home. I also wanted some cake to drown my drunken sorrows in.

Chapter Sixteen

Frosted Tits and Puke

Schuyler

The minute I walked in the door, I knew this was going to be one of those nights. I might rue it, I might regret it, but it was going to be one of those nights. In order to get in, I had to walk down a long, high corridor with granite flooring and an arched ceiling. Statues stood on both sides, the kind of delicate-looking, obviously expensive art figures that made me nervous. Things like half of a woman's face in polished black onyx, five feet high. A golden greyhound on a jade and marble pedestal. A huge square painting of what appeared to be geometric splatters in a simple museum-grade smoky chrome frame with a spotlight on it. Tasteful, muted, indirect lighting installed along the walls. The sounds of a party with youngish demographics came from the end, around the corner. I didn't want to be impressed, I resisted being impressed, but I was impressed. Who has a hallway like this? Most of the people I know live in apartments with fewer square feet than this hallway. It was ridiculous.

A girl walked by wearing nothing but a lacy bra and a pair of thong panties. I couldn't help myself; I turned around and continued to watch as she walked away. Who knows? Maybe tonight would become my newest and most reliable go-to when I'm touching myself, but one way or another, I could tell I was never going to forget it.

For one thing, the condo itself was amazing. I had never seen anything like it. As I rounded the corner, I could see that it had a heated indoor swimming pool (not a big one, but big enough) and a hot tub that could hold four people if they were being casual or six people who didn't mind a lot of close contact.

The pool/hot tub area had its own bar with a sink, a rack of glasses that included everything from tumblers to champagne flutes, a beer fridge, and a huge free-standing wine cooler with separate compartments for reds and whites, each with its own glass door. People were simply helping themselves.

"Hey man, you need a drink! What can I get for you?"

At first, I thought he was a bartender, but I swiftly realized that he was just a guy at that early, happy stage of being lightly drunk, and he was taking it upon himself to pass out other people's booze. I asked him for a rum & Coke, which he quickly and expertly produced, handing it to me with a flourish, a stir, a wedge of lime, and a napkin. I nodded thanks and continued to walk.

People were walking around in a mix of bathing suits, semiformal attire, underwear, and T-shirts. Chrissy, apparently, was acquainted with someone who knew a guy who worked with a person who was always invited to these parties. The guy who owned the condo was a software developer who had started and then sold at least three companies. He had a lot of friends.

That wonderful mix of alcohol and warm water was working its magic, and the nudity factor was escalating rapidly. A couple of the girls in the pool were already topless, and you could tell by the tone and inflection of their laughter that it wouldn't be much longer before those bottoms came off.

"Excuse me," a girl said as she brushed past me. "Sorry!"

I mumbled something along the lines of, "Don't worry about it," but when I turned, I did a double take. Her arm was in a cast, supported in a sling. She smiled apologetically. "Sorry! I feel like a bulldozer, pushing through a crowd with this thing. It's like I'm a mile wide and made of cement."

I felt a vigorous and sturdy erection quickly developing. "What, uh, what happened?" I asked, doing my best to sound offhand, staring at the cast. She was wearing a V-neck top with a ruffle, which highlighted her impressive cleavage.

"It was the dumbest thing! I was in Vail skiing, and I fell. They always tell you, let go of the pole, let go of the pole, but did I let go of the pole? No, I held on to it, and it dug into the snow, and I felt the bone in my arm go pop, just like *that*. It was so gross." She smiled at me. Her eyes didn't quite focus on me at the same time.

I backed up against a wall to catch my breath. This was too much. Just then, a girl walked by carrying a huge cake. CONGRATULATIONS PETER was written on it in professionally executed icing letters, surrounded by an elaborate border of icing flowers and stars. She had muscular arms and shoulders, well displayed in a tiny white ribbed cotton tank top over a dark red bra. She smiled at me.

"Need . . . er, any help with that?" I offered.

"No, I think I'm good. But thanks anyway." She carefully maneuvered her way into the kitchen—the kind of kitchen that could be on the cover of an interior design magazine—and gently set it down on the enormous granite counter of the center island. An assortment of stainless steel spatulas, ladles, and whisks hung on a rack behind her.

"Oh, *shit!*" She straightened up, holding her arms out to the side in the universal sign for, *look what I've done.*

There was a blotch of green and blue icing on her left breast (on that region of her tank top, anyway), slightly smeared. She appraised the damage to the top of the cake, which was negligible, almost undetectable. She laughed and looked at me like I was a co-conspirator in on a private secret. She raised her finger to her lips in a *shh* motion. I tried to smile back in a no-big-deal way without being all weird and creepy, but I'm sure I looked like a dog being taunted with bacon. I thought my dick was going to explode. I have to get out of here, I thought, and whirled around to make my escape before I did something stupid, illegal, and/or humiliating. But I when I did, I whirled right into Chrissy.

"Hi, Schuyler," she slurred, a big lopsided smile on her face. "Glad you could make it. Isn't this place great? Can I have some of that?" She took my drink out of my hand before I could answer and drained it.

"Chrissy, this is . . . uh, the girl with the cake. Girl with the cake, this is Schuyler. And I'm Chrissy. Except no, other way around. I'm Schuyler, and no cake. So, hello."

"You have icing on your boob," Chrissy said. "Here, let me get that for you." She ripped a paper towel from the roll and ran it under some hot water from the faucet.

"I'm sure she doesn't need any help," I said, putting out my hand to put on Chrissy's shoulder, but she moved away before it could land.

"No, it's fine," said Cake Girl. She smiled in appreciation as Chrissy dabbed the icing off her tit, leaving a damp spot.

"You have such great boobs," Chrissy said. "I love your boobs. They're so firm and perky. I wish I had boobs like yours."

"What are you talking about?" Cake Girl rejoined in the expected polite refutation, "Your boobs are beautiful."

Chrissy grabbed her own chest with both hands and started kneading. "What, these? Oh, they're all right, I guess. But thank you. You're very sweet." She turned to look at me. "I need a drink. Will you get me a drink?"

"So anyway, hello."

"Hello! Will you get me a drink?"

"Sure. What do you want?"

Chrissy looked at me like she was just realizing that I was standing there. "You're actually kind of cute, in a nerdy kind of way, you know that?"

"Thank you. What kind of drink do you want?"

"I need to pee," Chrissy announced suddenly. "Will you come with me and watch my purse?"

"Where's the bathroom?" I asked Cake Girl, who pointed. She was drying her tit with a dish towel.

Chrissy dragged me down the hall in the direction Cake Girl had pointed. Just as we got to the door, it opened, and a guy and a girl came out. The girl was straightening her skirt. The guy, who looked a little smug, belched. They headed back to the party. "Come in with me," Chrissy said, pulling on my wrist.

"I don't really . . ." I said, but allowed her to lead me inside. I pulled the door closed behind us.

She staggered to the toilet and pulled down her jeans and underwear. "I don't know who he thinks he even is," she huffed, as if we were in the middle of a conversation, "showing up like that and being all, you know. I mean, what's that even all about? I don't even know. It's crazy. What an asshole." She leaned back and stretched. "I don't think he even knows what he's missing. You would hit this, wouldn't you?"

Her legs were spread wide open, and the stream of urine was clearly visible as it emerged from between her labia, trickling into the bowl. She had been recently waxed, I noticed, but not so recently that there wasn't a faintly visible elongated triangular region of stubble on her pale skin. She reached down and pulled up her top, not enough to reveal her tits, but far enough to expose her navel—as if her bellybutton were as interesting as her genitals.

"You like this?" she asked.

"Yes," I said, reeling.

"You can fuck me if you want."

That was more than I needed to hear. I grabbed her by the waist and lifted her up onto the sink counter. Chrissy was not a small person, and I am not a strong guy. This maneuver would not have been even remotely possible without her assistance, which I took as a further encouraging sign to help partially drown out the chorus of doubts. Her belt dangled from her jeans, which were bunched around her ankles. One shoe was lying sideways on the bathroom floor, and the other was still on her foot. This is such a bad idea, I thought, irrelevantly. Such a bad, bad idea.

"Here, put one of these on." She opened up her purse and reached in to fish around. It slipped from her fingers as she was rummaging, and it dropped to the floor. A dozen condoms tumbled out. She picked one up at random, ripped the package open, and held it out. My pants were already unzipped. She tried to roll it on, but I had to help her. I had barely finished getting it into place when she reached around behind my back and pulled me to her, using her other hand to guide me in. She was unbelievably wet. Just like that, implausibly, incomprehensibly, I was inside her. My brain could barely register the reality of the situation over the screaming urgency of my gonads.

She slumped back against the mirror and put one foot up against the toilet tank, moaning with what I hoped was desire. Maybe it was confusion, or annoyance, or nausea. I'd be lying if I said I cared that much. On an impulse, I reached down and started to stroke her clit with two fingers while I was thrusting. She made a noise that suggested to me it was a good thing.

Honestly, I had never tried that before. I had read about the technique in a magazine or a Tumblr blog or something. I wanted to try to get her top open, but it seemed like too much trouble, and I was in an increasing hurry, worried that she would change her mind or pass out, or than an asteroid would obliterate all life on the planet before I finished.

Chrissy screamed, she actually screamed, with what was probably pleasure, grabbing my hair with both hands. It was the sound of her voice that pushed me over the brink, and I felt the involuntary spasmodic convulsions shooting through my groin, the clumsy rocking in my pelvis, like my whole body was out of control. For a second, I wasn't even aware of Chrissy being there, even though I was still inside her. And then it was over. The world came back. Objects returned to focus. Colors flooded back. My awareness, my sense of time and place and logic and reason, seeped back into my brain. I pulled back and slipped out of her. I yanked off the condom with a snap and tossed it in the wastebasket. Chrissy was still wobbling, her eyes half closed, a faint smile on her face. "Oh Schuyler," she said, and then threw up all over me.

The rest of the evening was a grim blur of stumbling down to the street to hail a cab, getting her home, and then walking back to my place.

I knew better, dammit, I *knew* better! I wondered if I was going to be facing assault charges. Well, hell. I deserved it. Just when I thought I couldn't possibly be a bigger jerk, I proved myself wrong. What was I thinking? I wasn't thinking at all; that was the problem. Clarity surrounded me like a cruel affliction. I needed to get drunk. Or die. Or something.

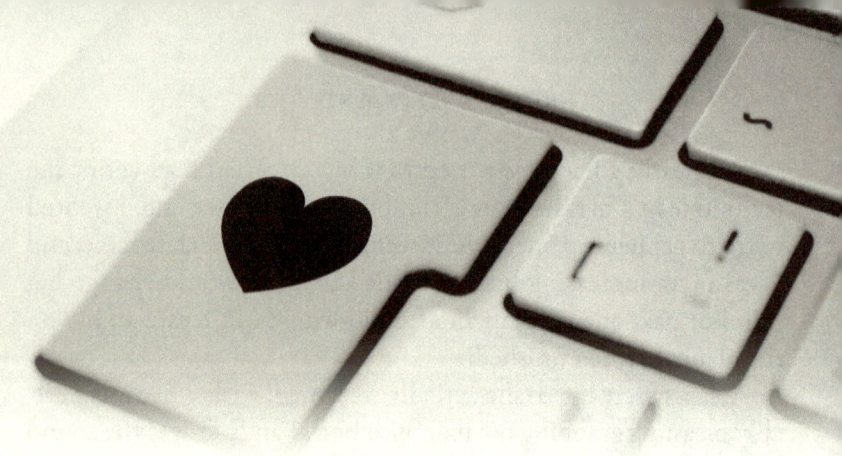

CHAPTER SEVENTEEN

The Trainwreck

CHRISSY

I woke up the next afternoon on the floor of my bathroom.

No idea how I got there.

My head felt like a basketball filled with water. My throat burned, and my stomach felt like at any moment it was going to tear out of my body like an alien.

My phone was going off somewhere in the distance. I tried willing it towards me and nothing happened.

I needed a shower.

First I needed to assess how bad the situation was. I sat up and immediately regretted the motion. I wanted to die. It had to be less painful.

After a couple of minutes of slow breathing, I found that I was mostly dressed which also meant that I was covered in multi-color vomit. So was the floor, the toilet, and the bathroom rug. I was happy to discover that it was not also all over the tub.

It took me some time, but I was finally able to use towels, clothing, and toilet paper to clean up the vomit enough to get it to the washing machine. I dreaded seeing the rest of the apartment because if there was vomit everywhere, I might just burn the entire place down.

Luckily, if I can say that given the circumstances, the damage was contained to the bathroom.

I put all the towels, rugs, and clothes in the washer and then peeled off the ones I was wearing. This was a disgusting mess.

As I pulled off my panties, I saw it. I would like to say that I should have felt it first. The full feeling, even if you haven't eaten anything, but I didn't.

The panties however told another story completely. I had sex last night.

My heart sank.

Had I let Mitchell fuck me again?

I really needed a shower now.

I put all the clothes in washer, started the load, and headed into the shower as hot as I could take it.

As the water turned from hot to cold, I knew I was stalling. A huge part of me wanted to pretend whatever happened and whomever I did the whatever with would evaporate from my mind.

I even found myself begin to wonder if I should drink away this problem only to get really queasy again.

Shutting the shower off, I bundled up and went in search of the phone. It hadn't been alerting me further or I had simply tuned it out. When I found it finally on the floor with my purse and shoes, it was out of charge. I plugged it in and went in search of something to make the idea that I would continue to dry-heave less.

About fifteen minutes later, I checked the phone. I scrolled through the text messages and phone calls and there it was. I had texted Schuyler. Before I began to read what it said, I closed my eyes and silently swore to myself.

There really should be an app that allows you to mark certain numbers that shouldn't be contacted when you are drinking. Of course, how in the hell would the phone know you had ingested alcohol? My brain hurt.

I scrolled. There were three messages.

"Hey. U up?"

"Com 2 parrty and git me (insert address)"

"(Re-typed address) Srry. Drriunk."

Now I was actually hoping I had hooked up with Mitchell again. I put the phone down and decided to get dressed. In my PJs at least.

Knowing I had sex, knowing there was a chance it was with Schuyler, and knowing there was a chance it was unprotected made me want to scream.

Looking at the fact it would have been better for me to get completely loaded in my apartment by myself versus this. I walked into the living room and found a note on the table.

"Hope you are ok," signed S.

I was staring at the note when it hit me: I was surrounded by work colleagues and they may have seen who I fucked. I almost said that this couldn't possibly get worse, but I didn't want to jinx myself.

I picked up the phone again and quickly typed a text and put it down. Then picked it up again and continued typing. Every angry thought came out in several misspelled venomous texts and insults.

Well at least I knew. I edited Schuyler's contact to add back the X with the hope I never made that mistake again. I hope he used a condom. Fuck.

I shut down my Seraphim after buying a plan B pill, just in case. Then I spent the rest of the weekend in my apartment and used my remaining sick and vacation days to take the next week off.

I took a train up to see Jess and spent some time walking through the galleries trying to remind myself why I was here in the city and remember my dream of something in the art world.

Whether I was mentally blocking the last couple of months, or somehow I found some kind of inner peace after eating almost nothing but ice cream, I will never know. However, near the end of the week, I found myself no longer dwelling on mistakes. Maybe I was in a better place.

That Friday night Sean #3 sent me a text asking if I wanted to grab a drink. I hesitated for a moment before replying "Yes." He told me what bar to meet him at and the time. I got all dressed up, feeling pretty great about the person looking back at me in the mirror.

As I walked towards the bar, I scrolled up through his texts to find the dick pics he had been sending me for months.

This night might just get a little better after all.

Chapter Eighteen

Missing The Frosting

Schuyler

I've been rejected before. Hell, I've been rejected lots of times. Rejected is basically all I've ever been. But never before in my life had I been so roundly and robustly kicked to the curb, hurled straight into the dating dumpster.

I immediately pounded out a ferocious response to her text, typing so fast my hands were cramping, rebutting every allegation point by point. My logic was irrefutable; my conclusions were iron-clad. I included footnotes and a cross-referenced index with multiple appendices and a full list of references cited. I may have used the words "cunt" and "whore" a bit more often than necessary.

My thumb hovered over the SEND button. I hesitated. Then, after a long and thoughtful pause, I tapped DELETE.

I fell backwards into bed with all my clothes on. With one last agonized creak, the bedframe finally failed, and the mattress collapsed to the floor, lopsided and askew. The impact of my body weight shook the room and caused the lamp to fall over, breaking the bulb, and leaving me in darkness. "Shut the fuck up in there," yelled Mean Roommate, beating on the wall with his fist.

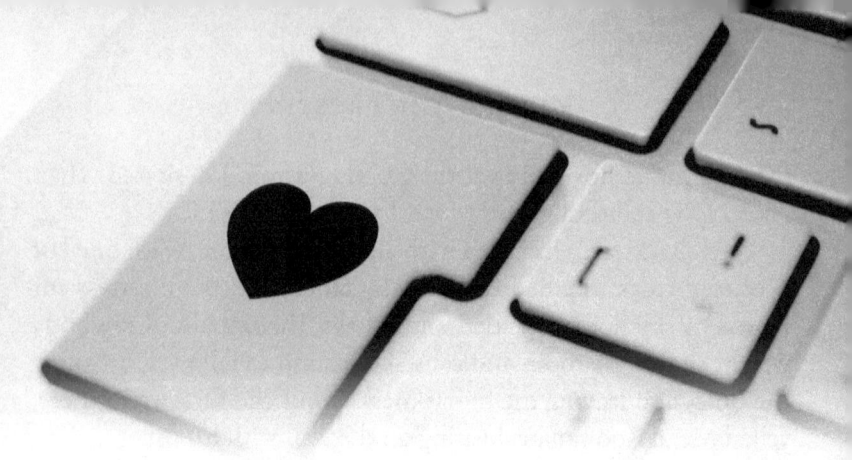

Epilogue

One Year Later

Schuyler

I was at a bar on Amsterdam Avenue when I bumped into a guy.

"Sorry," I mumbled, getting out of his way.

"No problem," he said, then stopped and looked at me. "Schuyler?"

"Yeah," I said, squinting at him. There was an uncomfortable moment as he smiled at me. I had no idea who he was. Then it hit me. "Shay? Oh my *God*, is that *you*?"

"It's Shawn now. But yeah. It's me. How the hell are ya, Sky-man?"

"I don't know what to say."

"It's OK, bro." Shawn slapped me on the shoulder. "Nobody ever does. It's cool. You'll get used to the idea."

"Should I say . . . um, congratulations? Or is that weird?"

"You can say whatever you want. Listen, man. I'm glad you're here. I owe you an apology. I've been thinking about this for a long time. I was a dick to you because I was confused about things, and that wasn't fair. I'm sorry." He extended his hand and I shook it. "We cool?"

"Yeah. We're cool."

I hurried home and turned on my computer. I keyed in the first three letters of the URL, and the rest of the address auto-populated. Jekyll's smiling face appeared.

"Hi, Schuyler!"

"Hi, Jekyll."

"How are you?"

"Honestly? Not great."

"I'm sorry to hear that."

I shrugged. "Forget it. How are you?"

"I'm . . ." Her smile cracked. "To tell you the truth, I'm not great, either."

We sat in silence for a moment.

"Want to know what I have?" She leaned in close to the Web cam like she was letting me in on a secret.

"Tell me."

She leaned back and reached for something. It was a cake. "Did you know I'm an English professor?"

"No, I didn't know that." I unzipped my pants.

"My students made me this. We're going to have a party today to celebrate the end of the semester."

"That sounds like fun," I said, reaching down with my right hand. "It's a nice cake. It sure would be terrible if anything bad happened to it."

ABOUT THE AUTHOR

So here is something about little ole me; I have had a very interesting upbringing, starting with growing up in Hollywood, CA. Never shy, I learned that if you are not willing to try something new, you may let life simply pass you by. I love meeting people from all walks of life and these experiences inspire me on a daily basis. As a true friend once pointed out "You are never a complete waste, you can always be used as a bad example." So, what's the worst that can happen?

www.DaliaLance.com
Twitter: @DaliaLance
Facebook.com/authordalialance

Don't forget to check out

the Randi Micheals Series

by Dalia Lance!

Discover more at
4HorsemenPublications.com

10% off using HORSEMEN10